MARGRET & H.A. REY'S

Curious George®

IN FOLLOW THAT HAT!

Houghton Mifflin Harcourt

Boston   New York

www.hmhco.com

Written by Liza Charlesworth
Illustrations by Fran Brylewska and David Brylewski
for Artful Doodlers Ltd.

ISBN 978-1-328-73718-2

Manufactured in China
SCP 10 9 8 7 6 5 4 3 2 1
4500702601

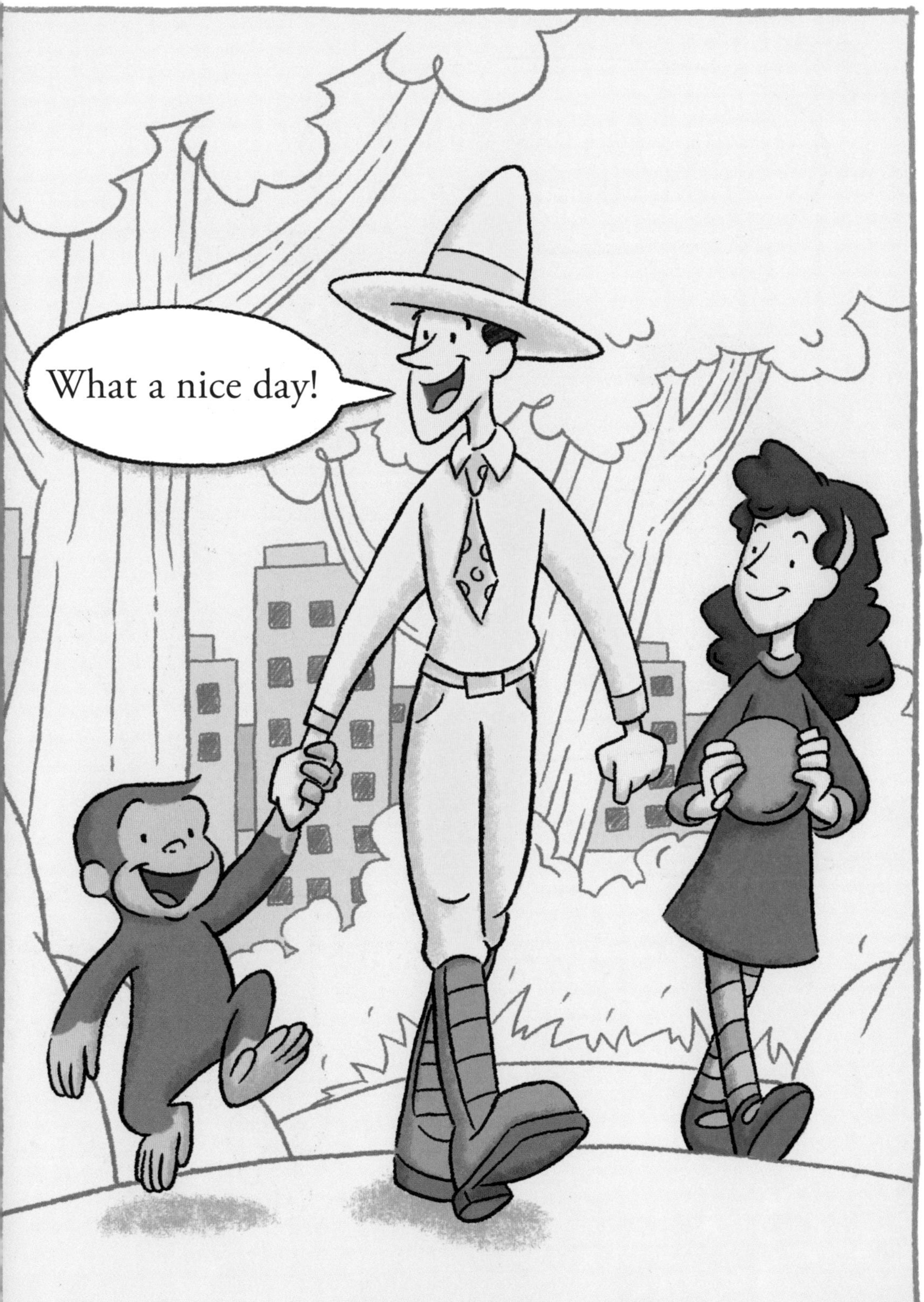
What a nice day!

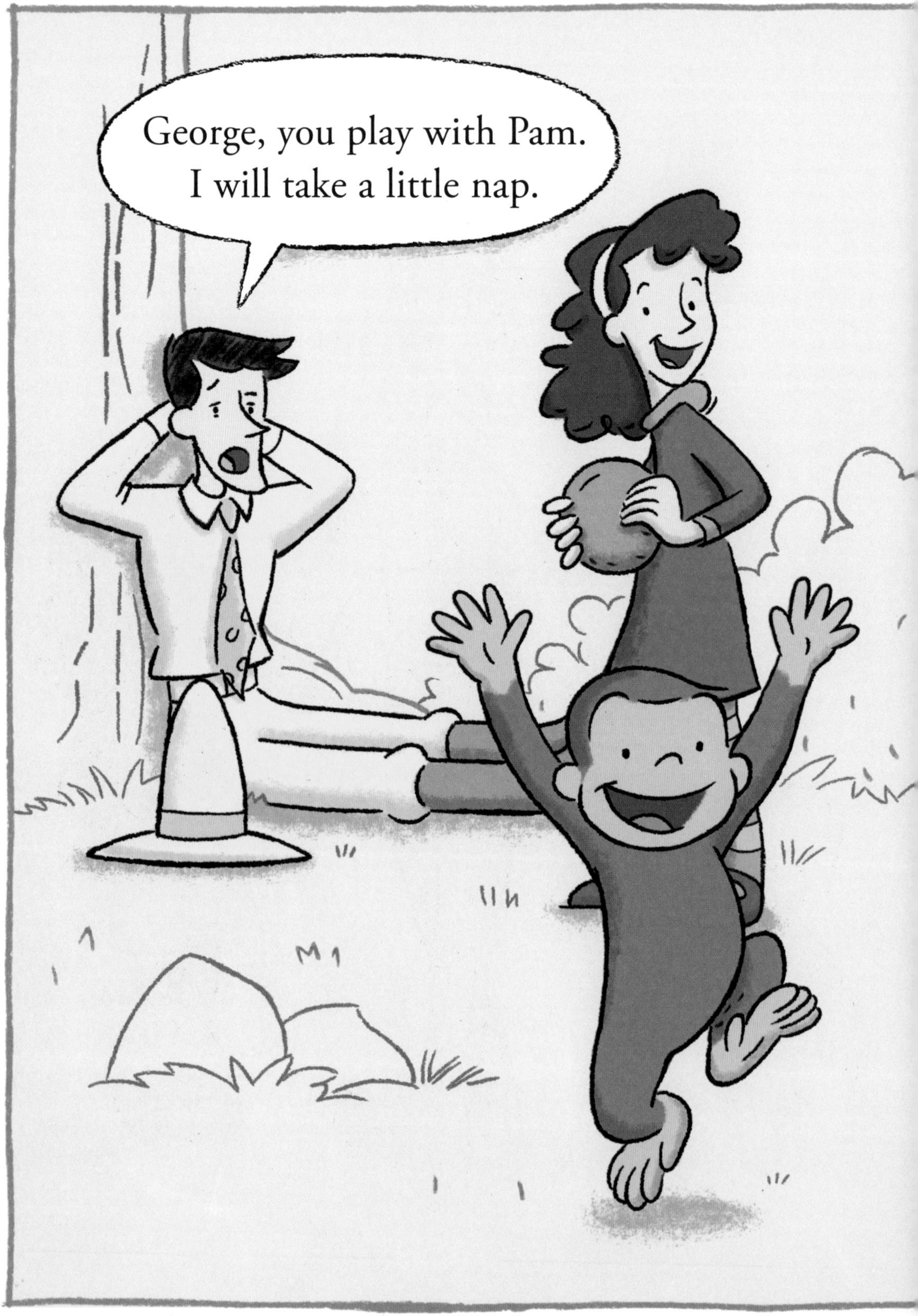
George, you play with Pam. I will take a little nap.

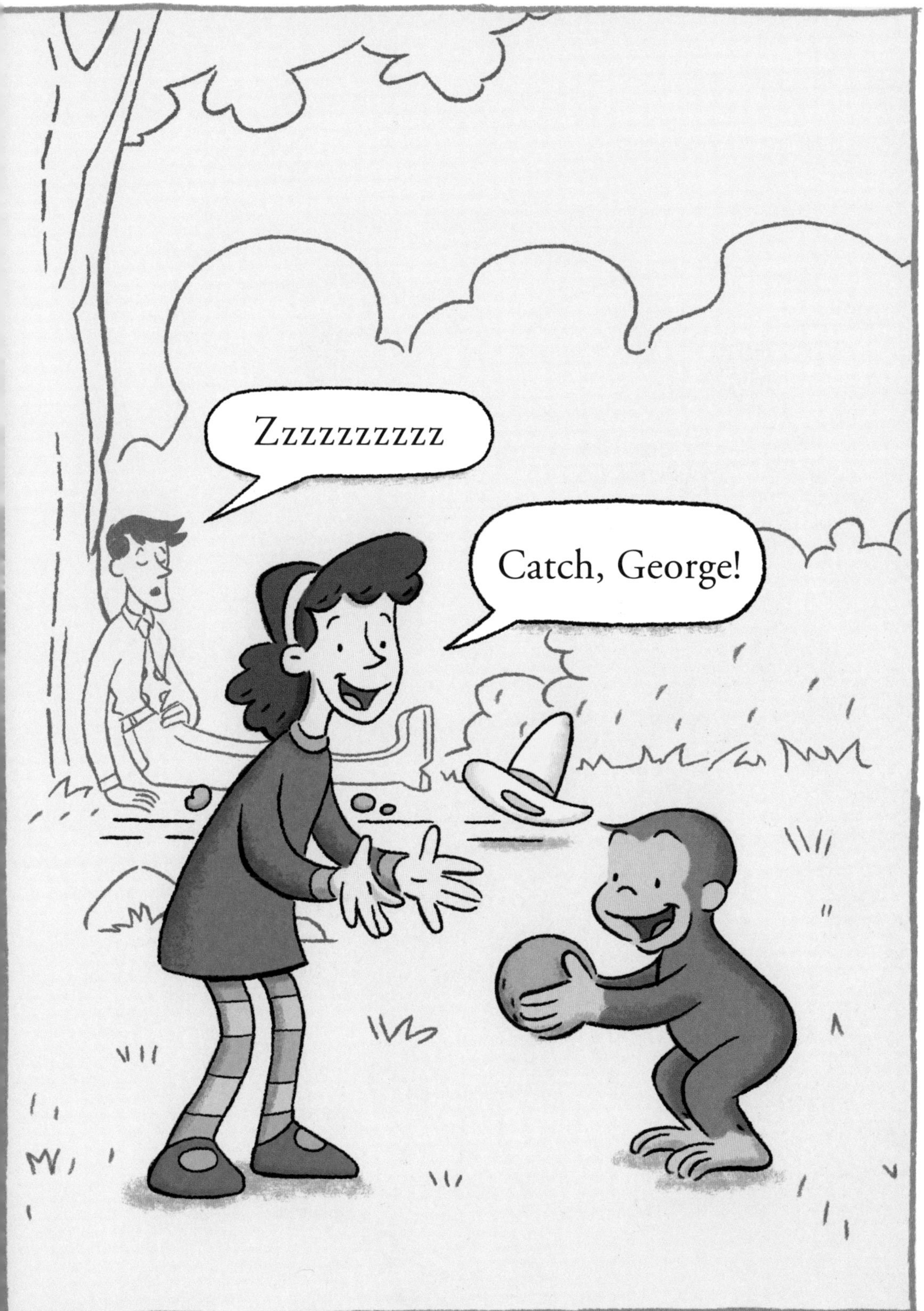
Zzzzzzzzzz
Catch, George!

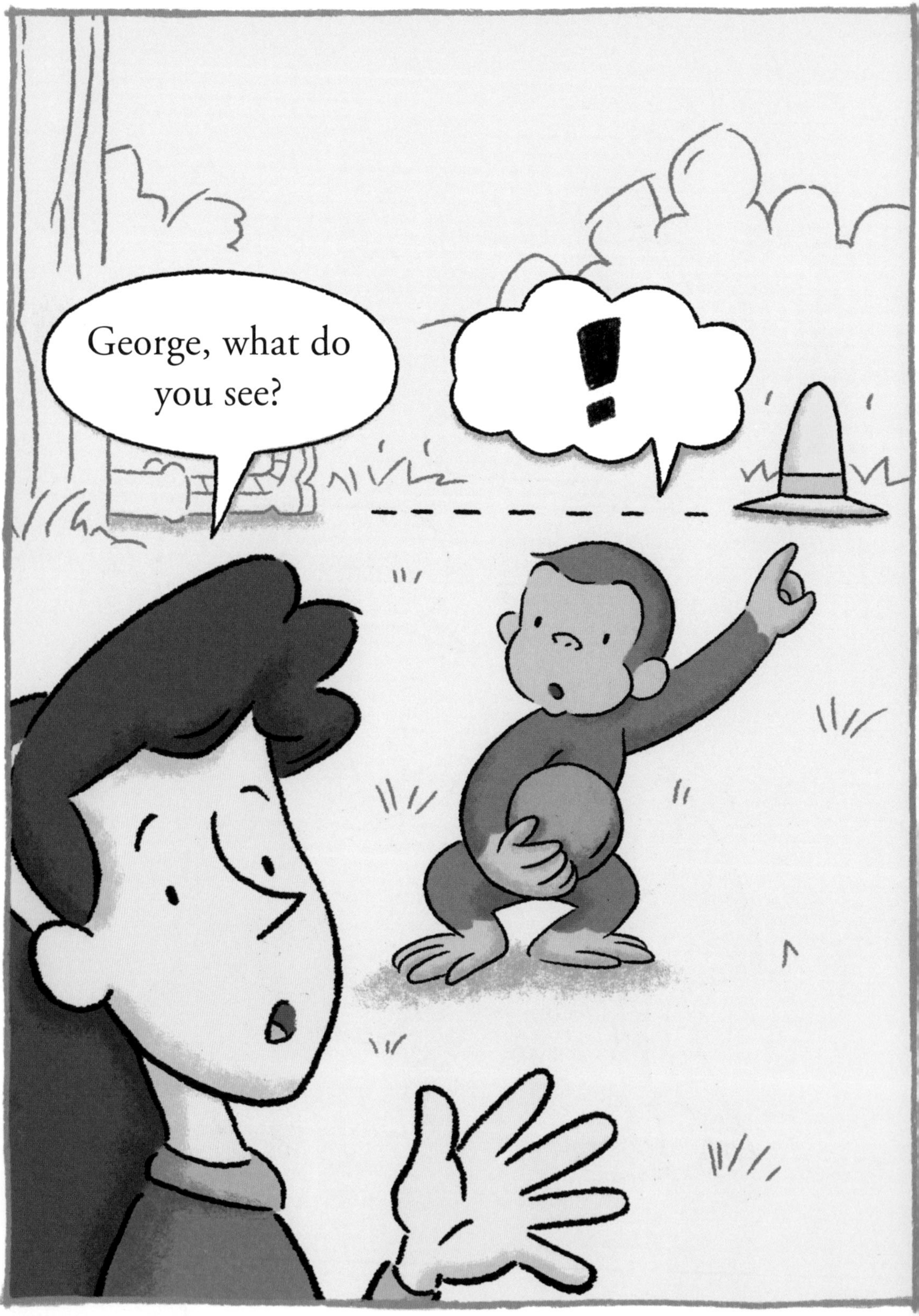
George, what do you see?
!

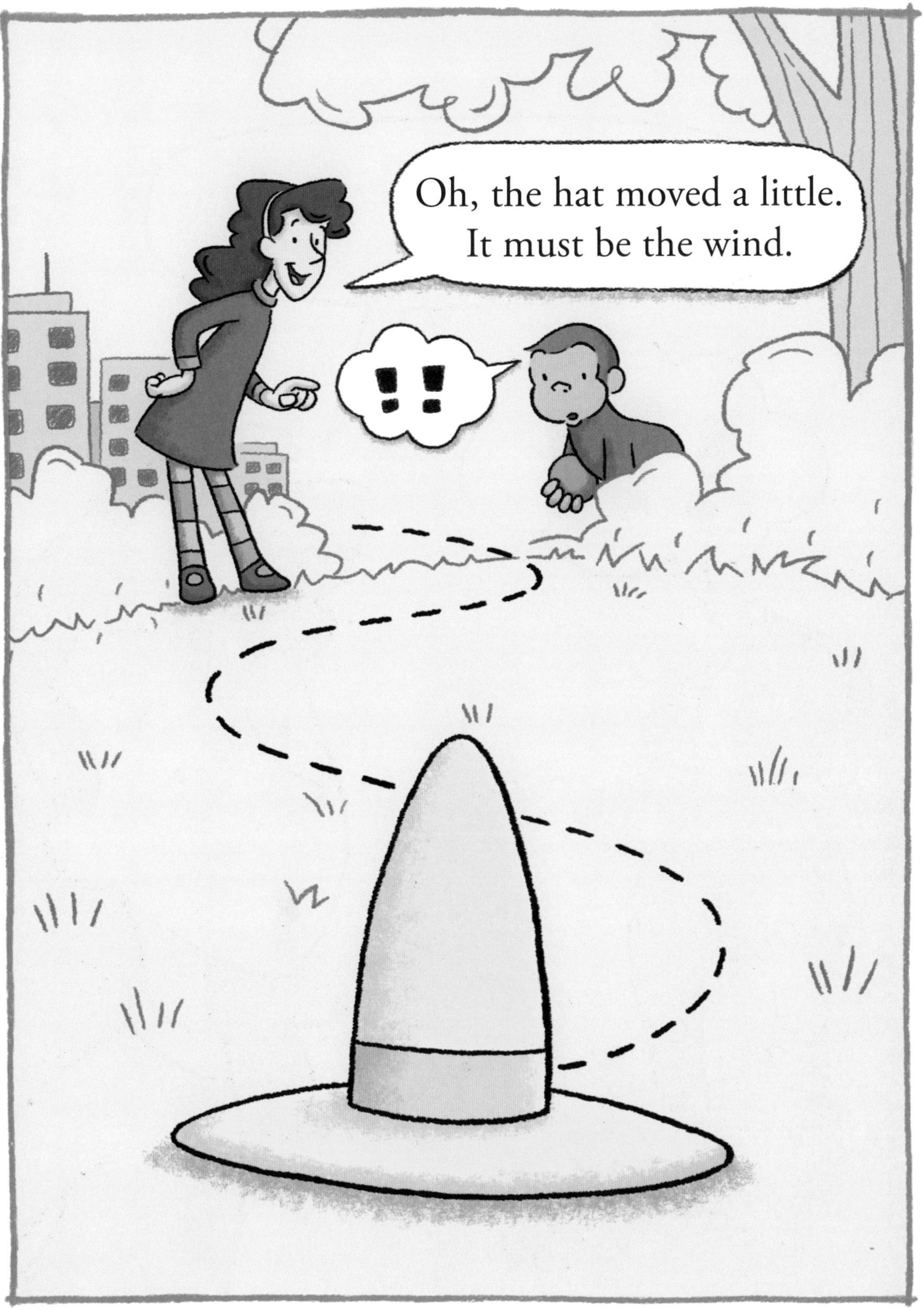
Oh, the hat moved a little. It must be the wind.
!!

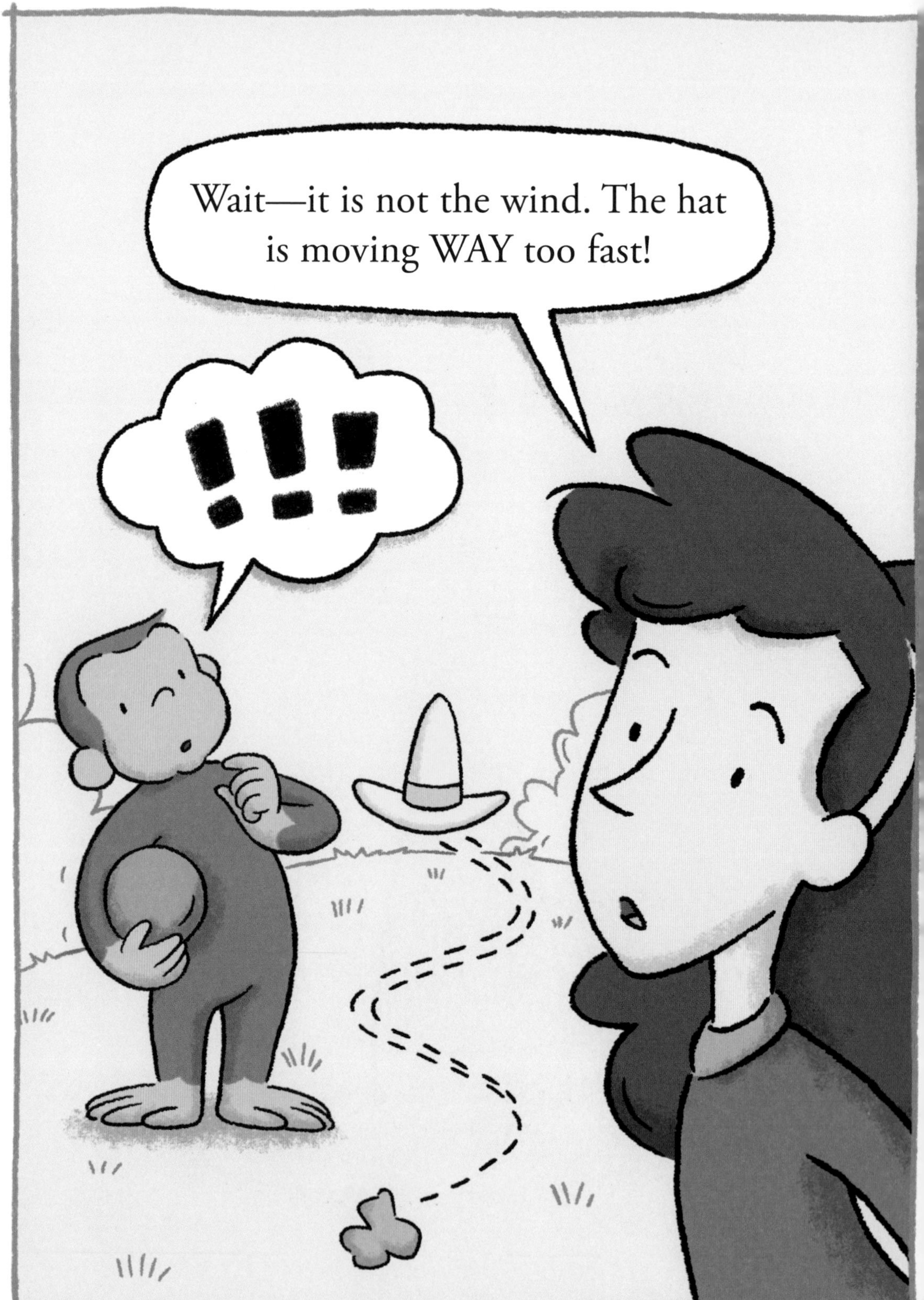
Wait—it is not the wind. The hat is moving WAY too fast!
!!!

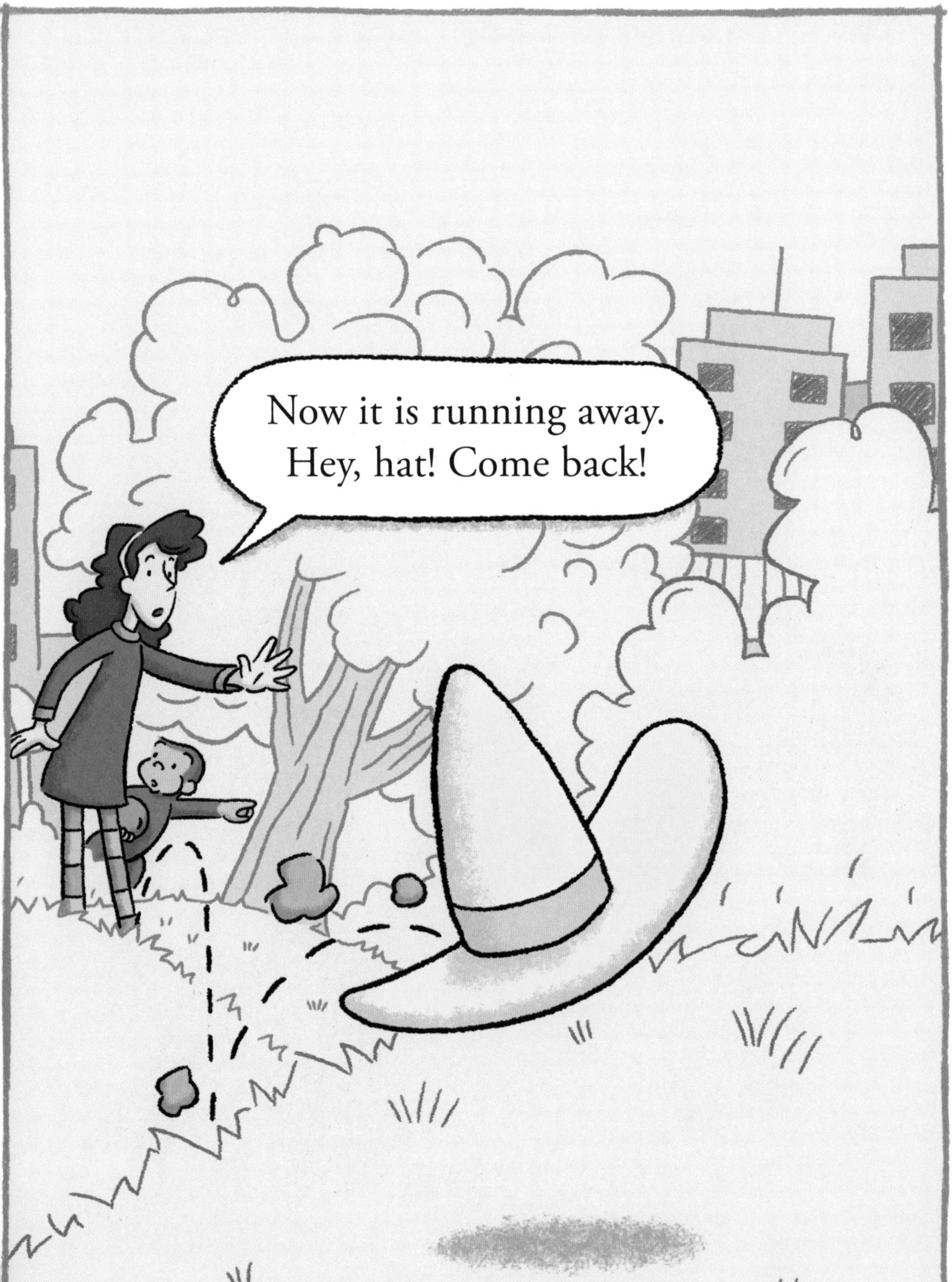
Now it is running away.
Hey, hat! Come back!

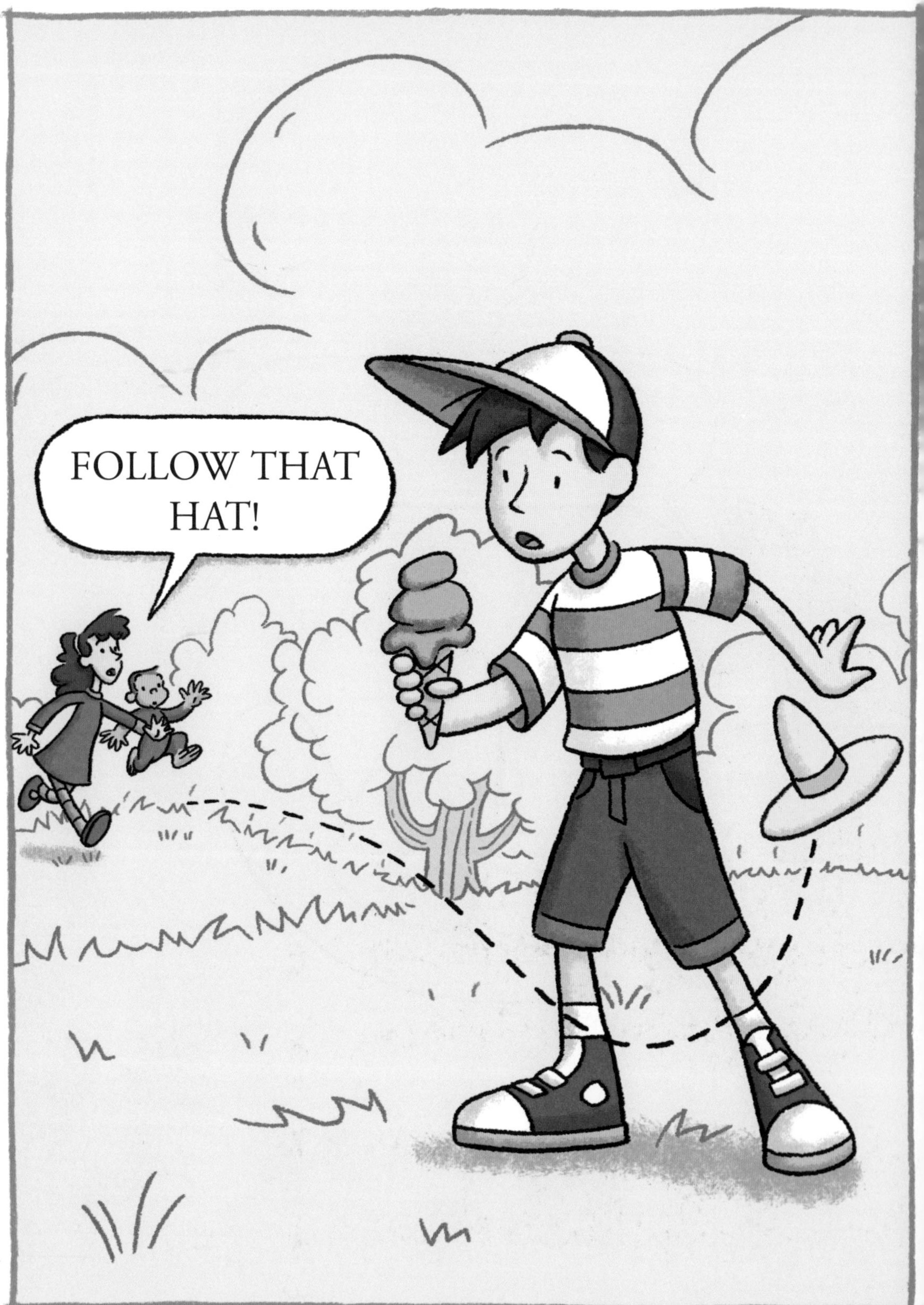
FOLLOW THAT HAT!

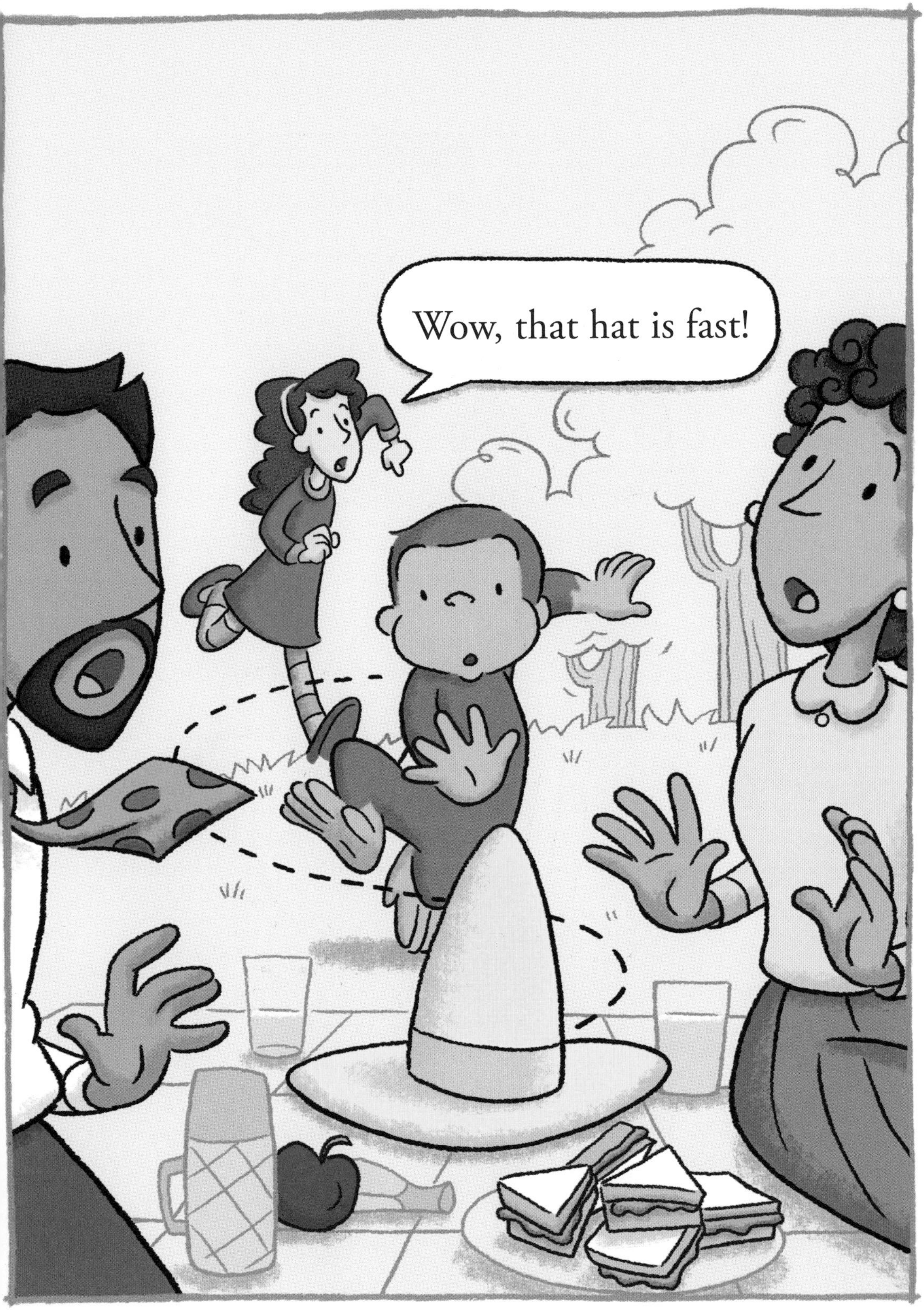
Wow, that hat is fast!

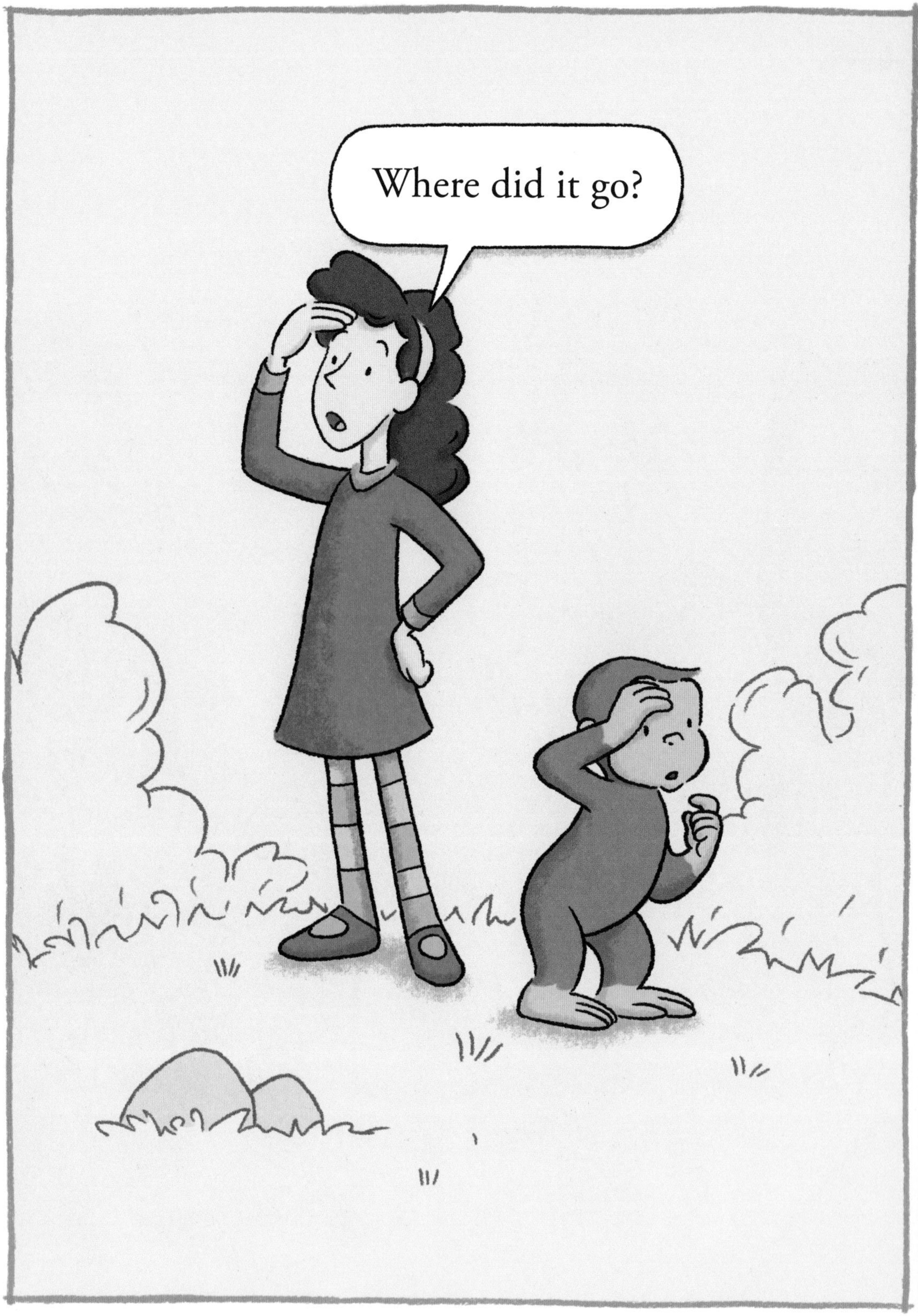
Where did it go?

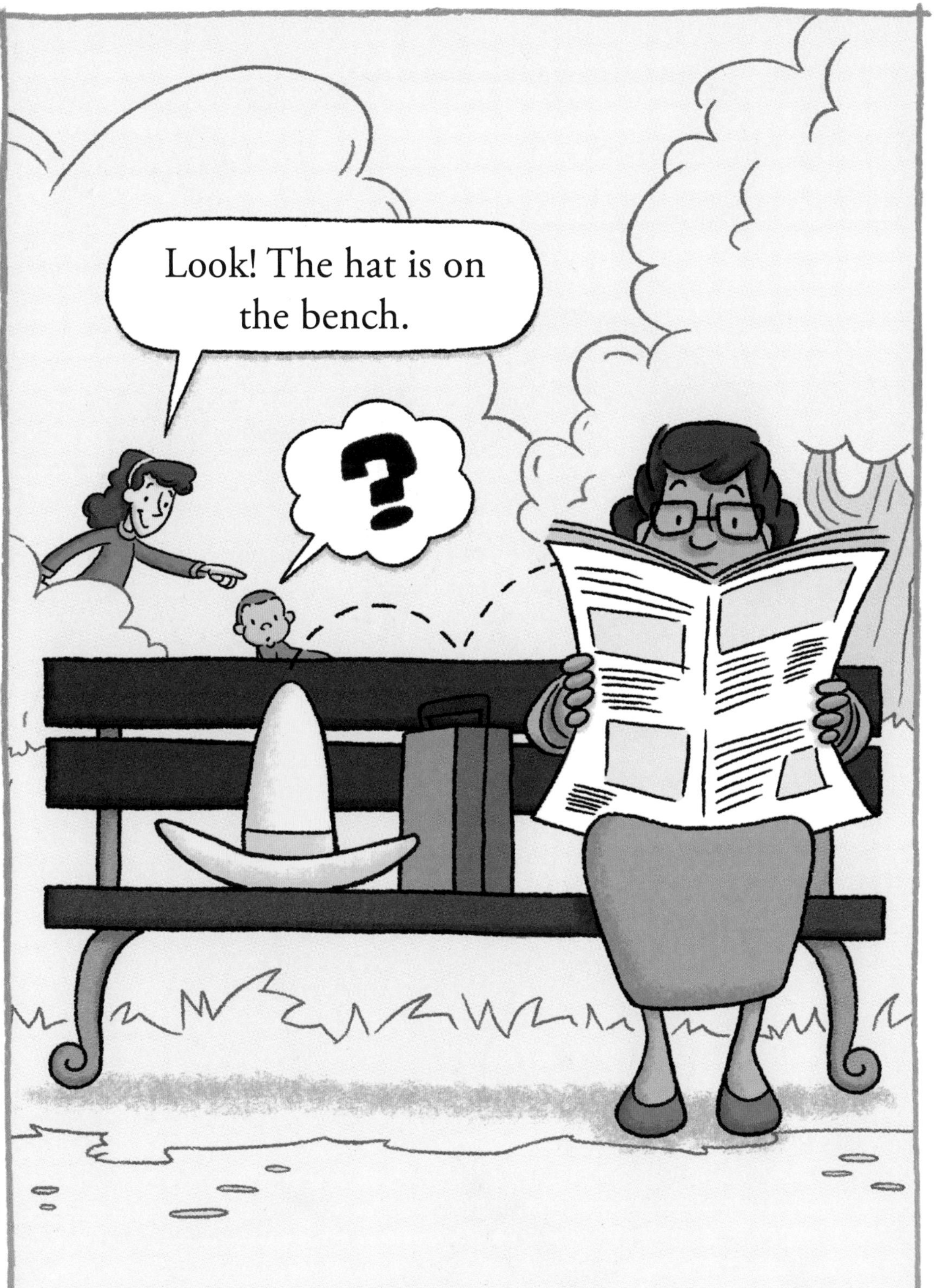
Look! The hat is on the bench.
?

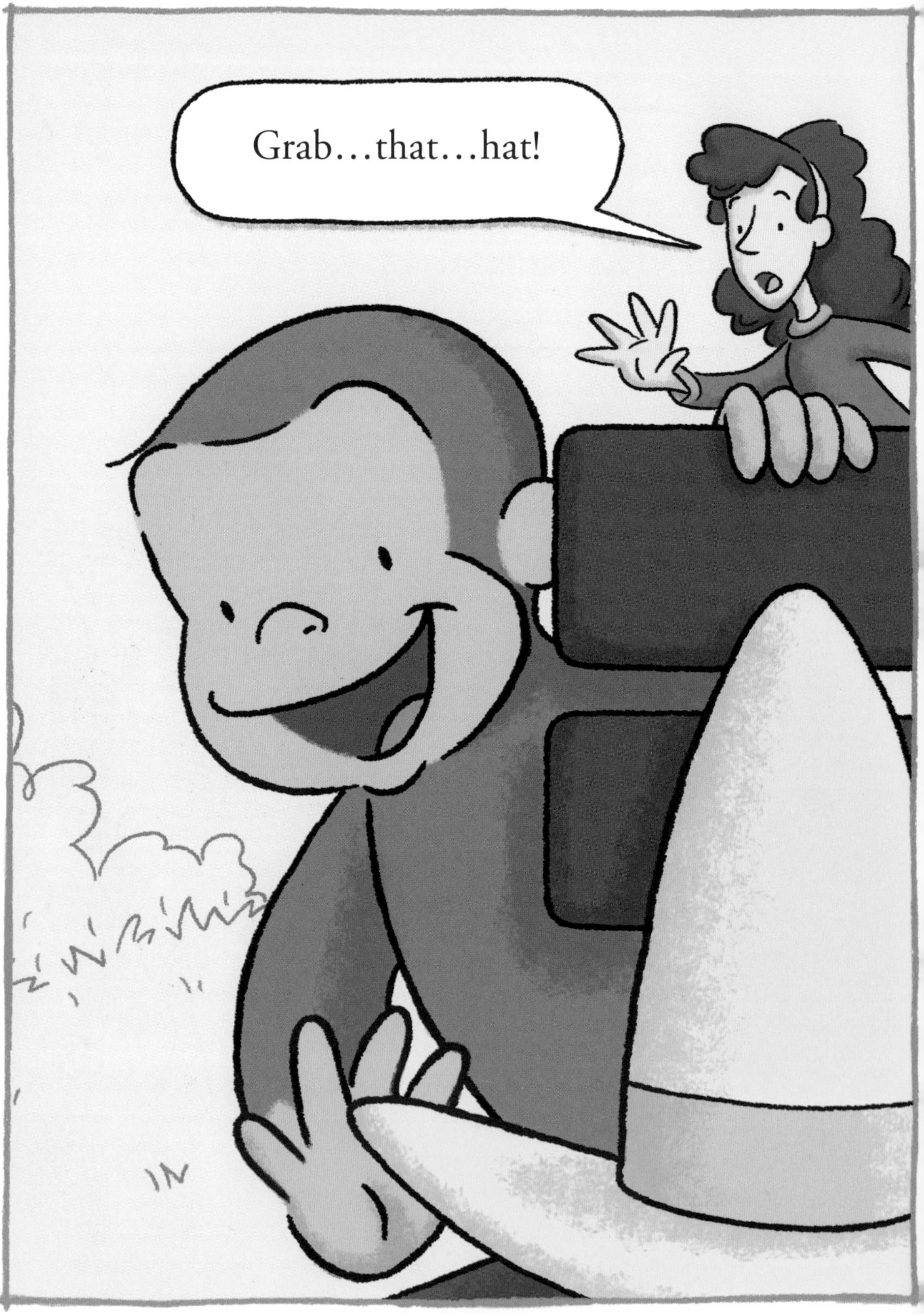
Grab…that…hat!

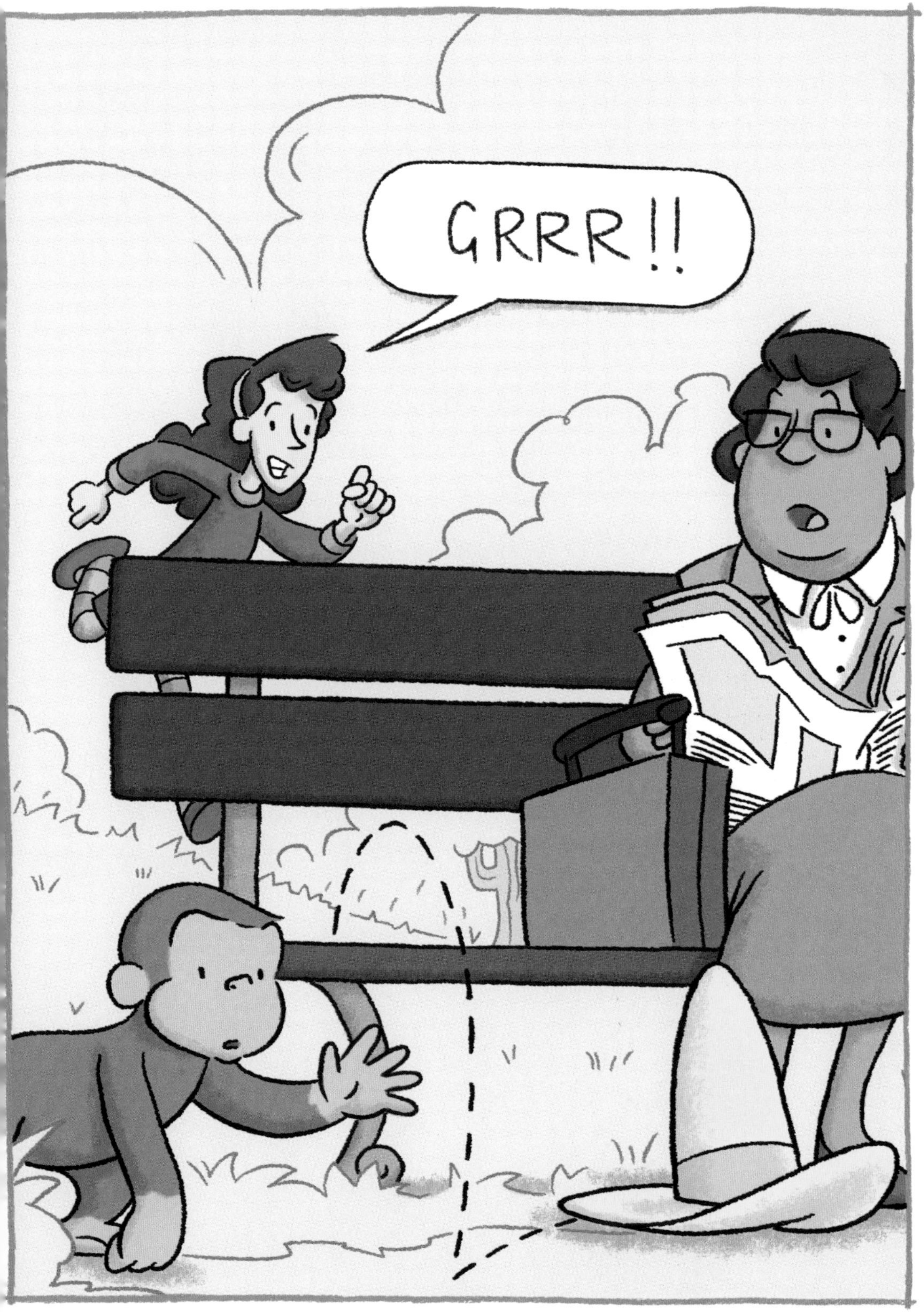
GRRR!!

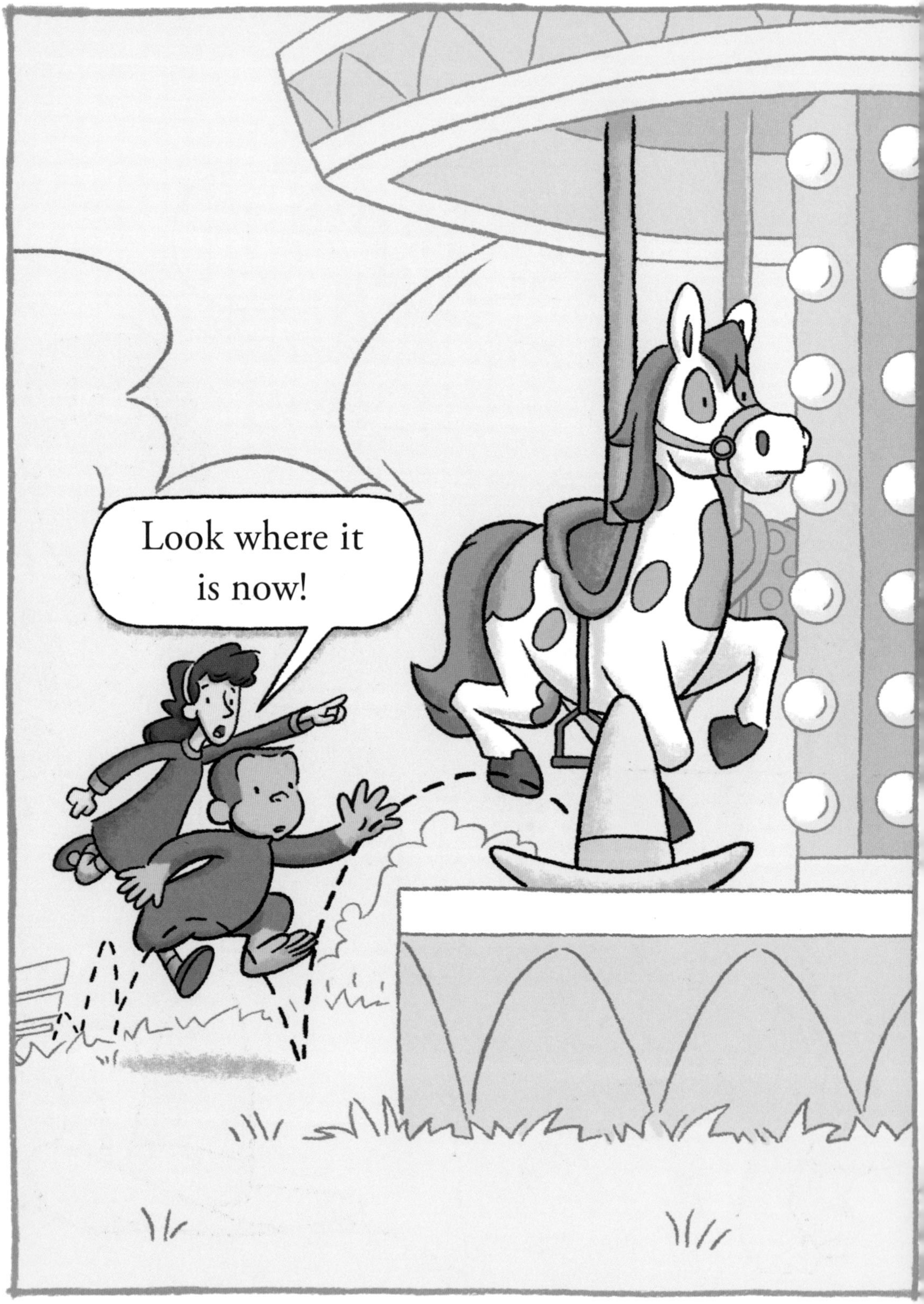
Look where it is now!

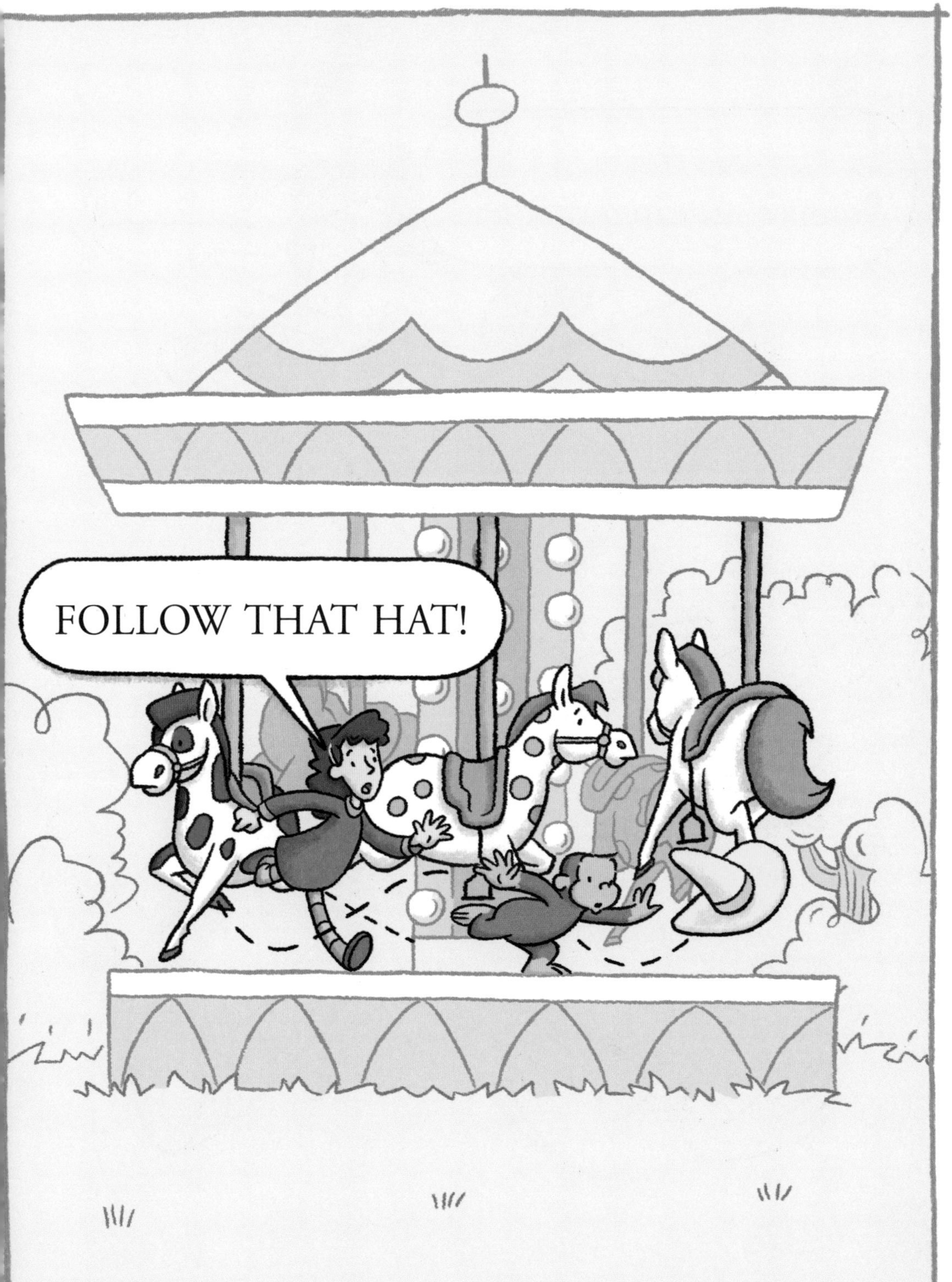
FOLLOW THAT HAT!

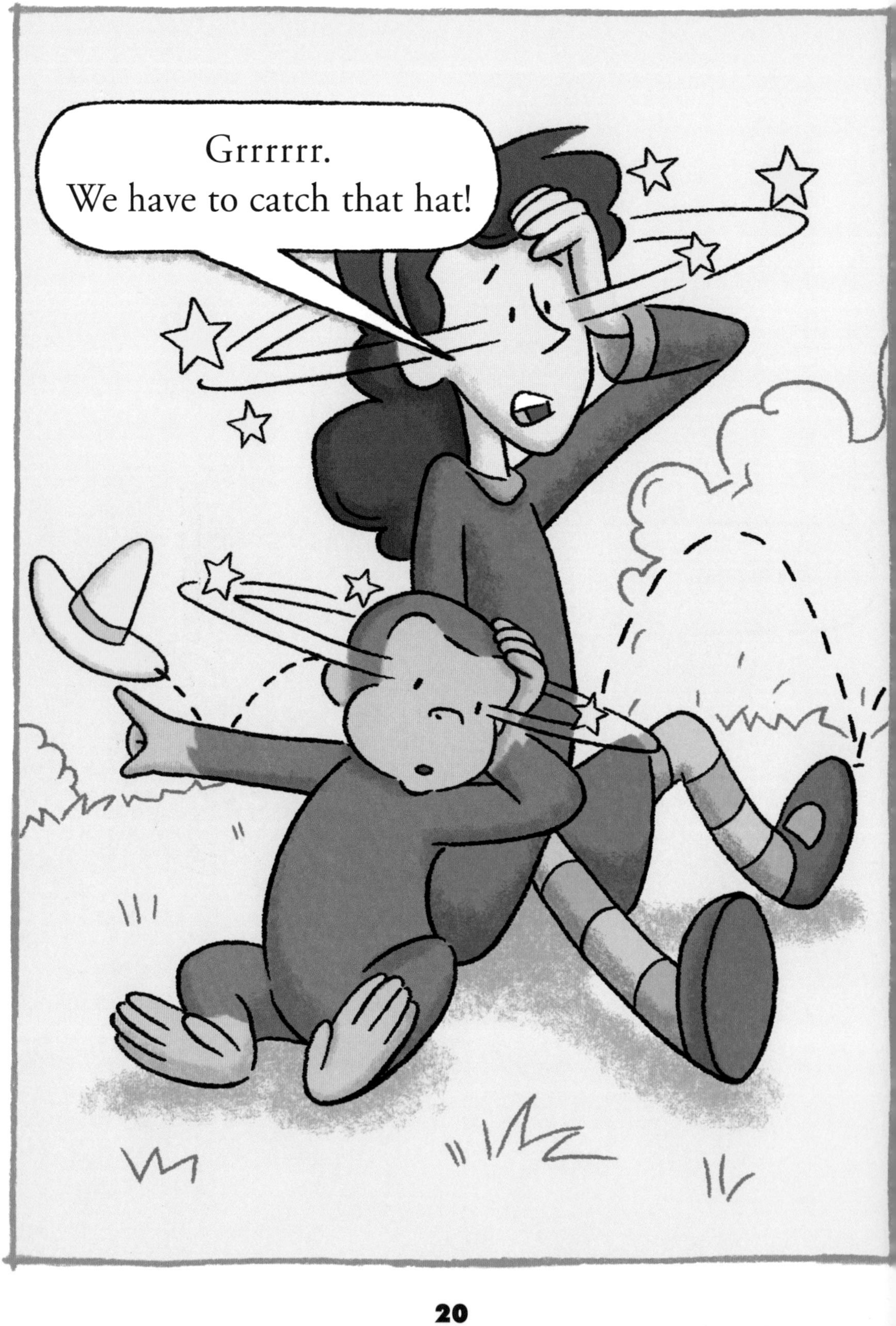
Grrrrrr.
We have to catch that hat!

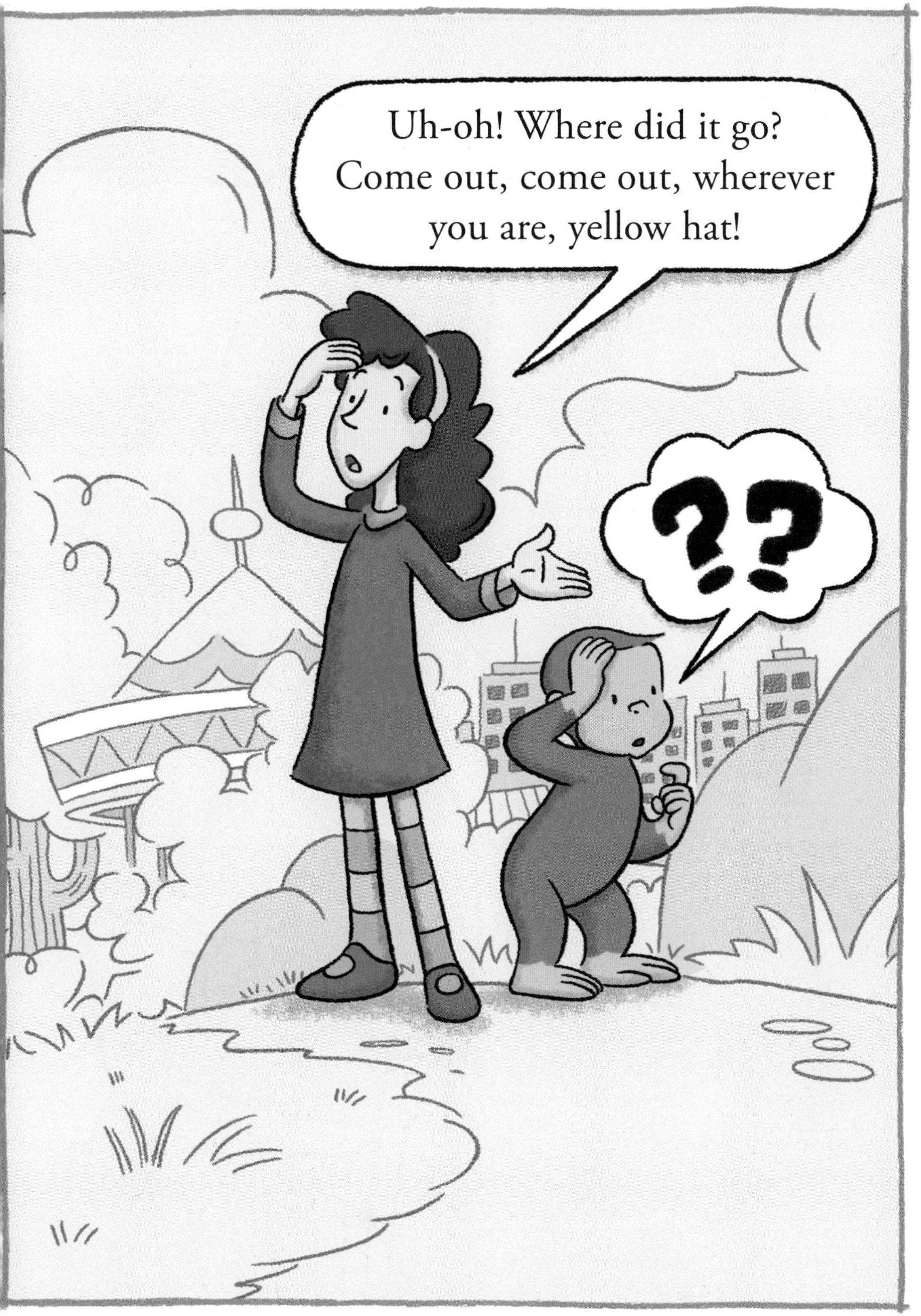
Uh-oh! Where did it go? Come out, come out, wherever you are, yellow hat!
??

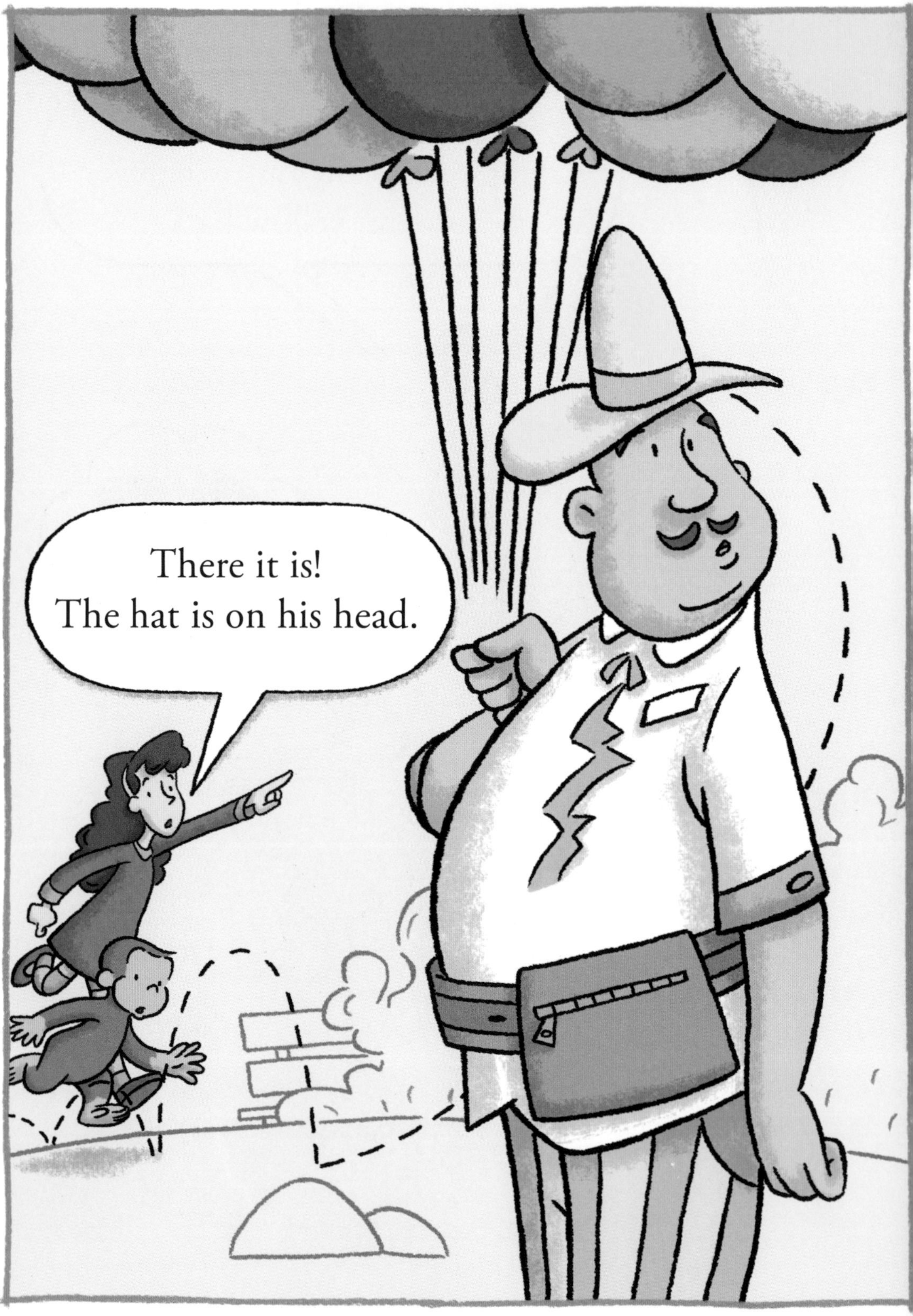
There it is!
The hat is on his head.

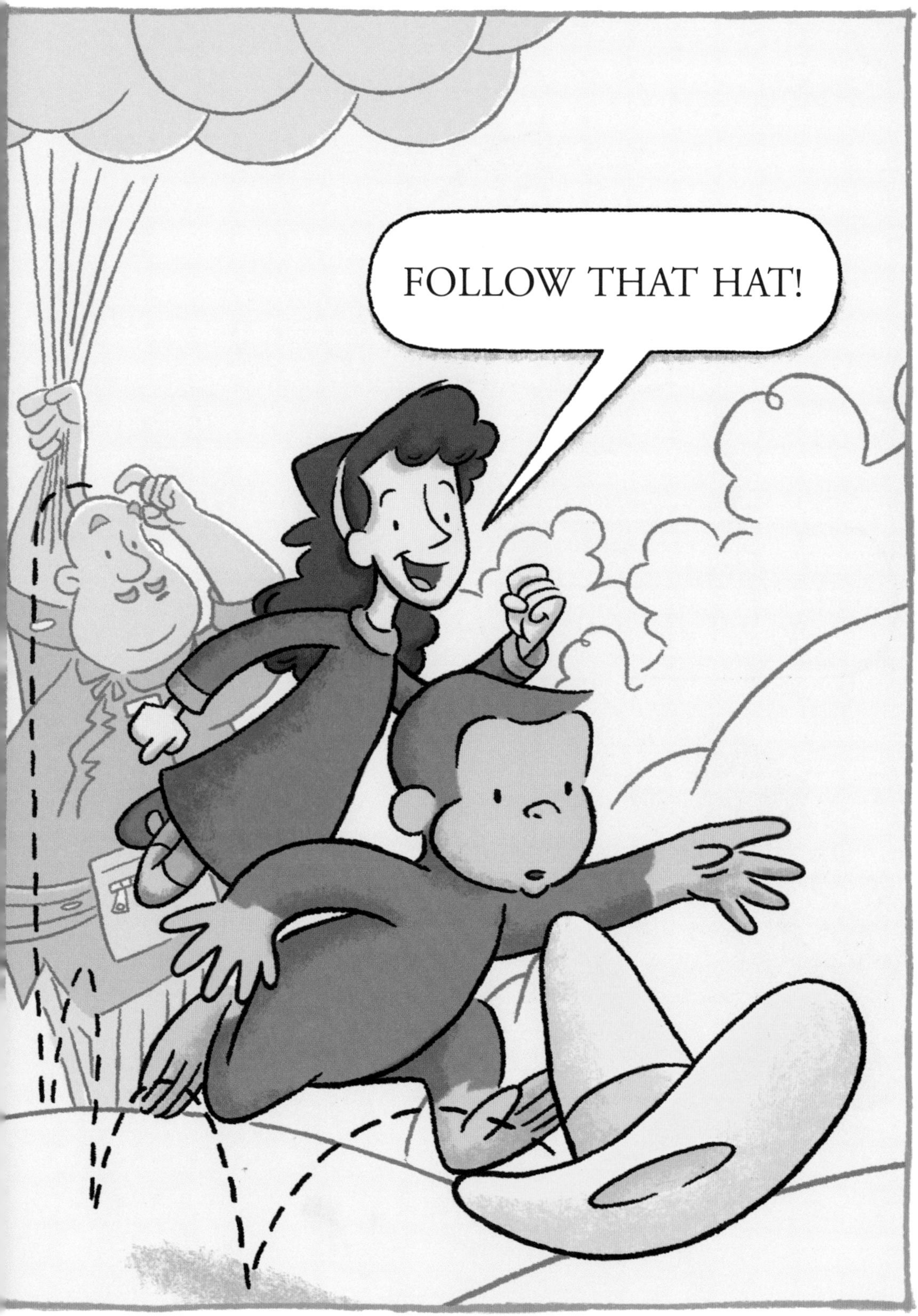
FOLLOW THAT HAT!

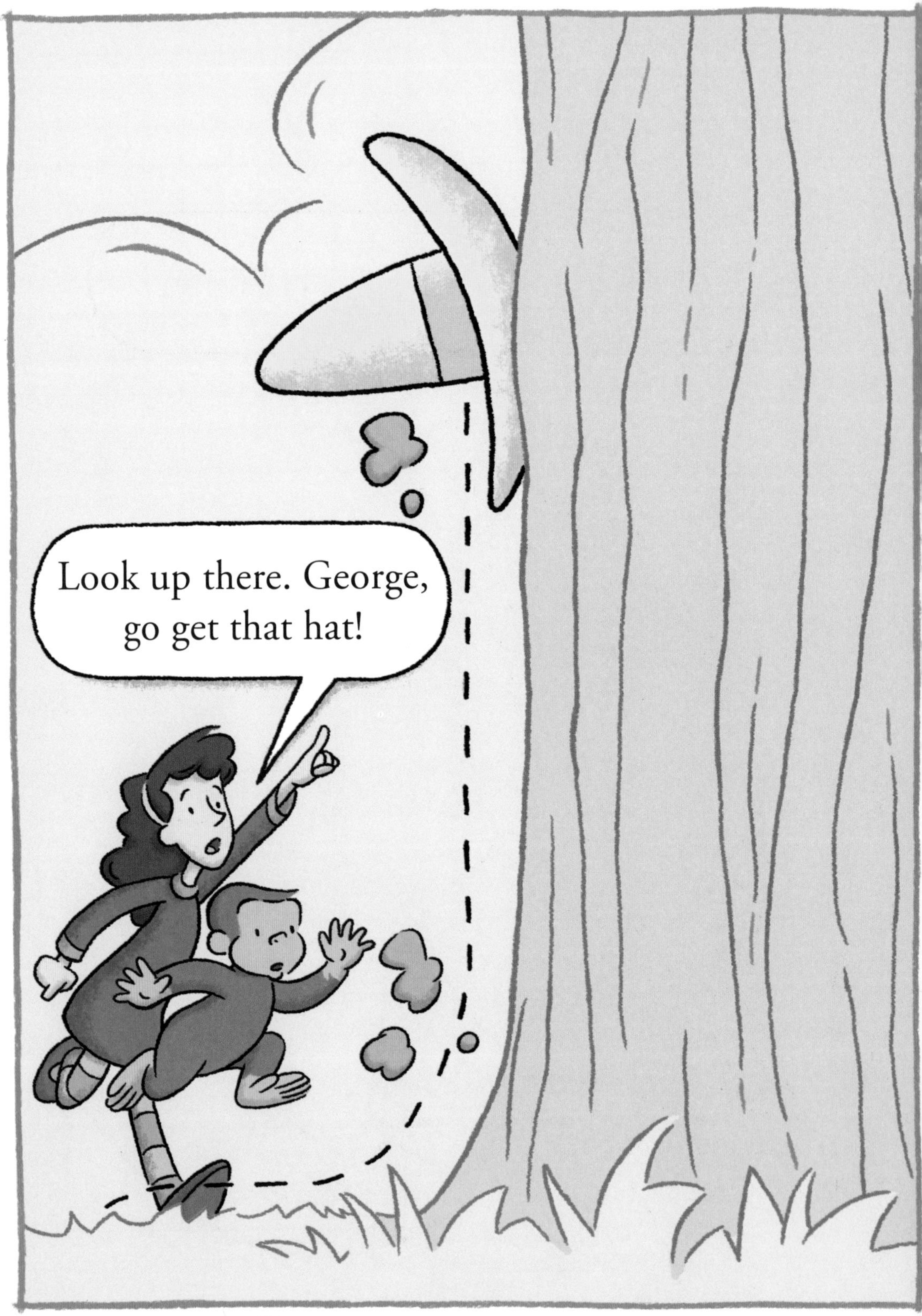
Look up there. George, go get that hat!

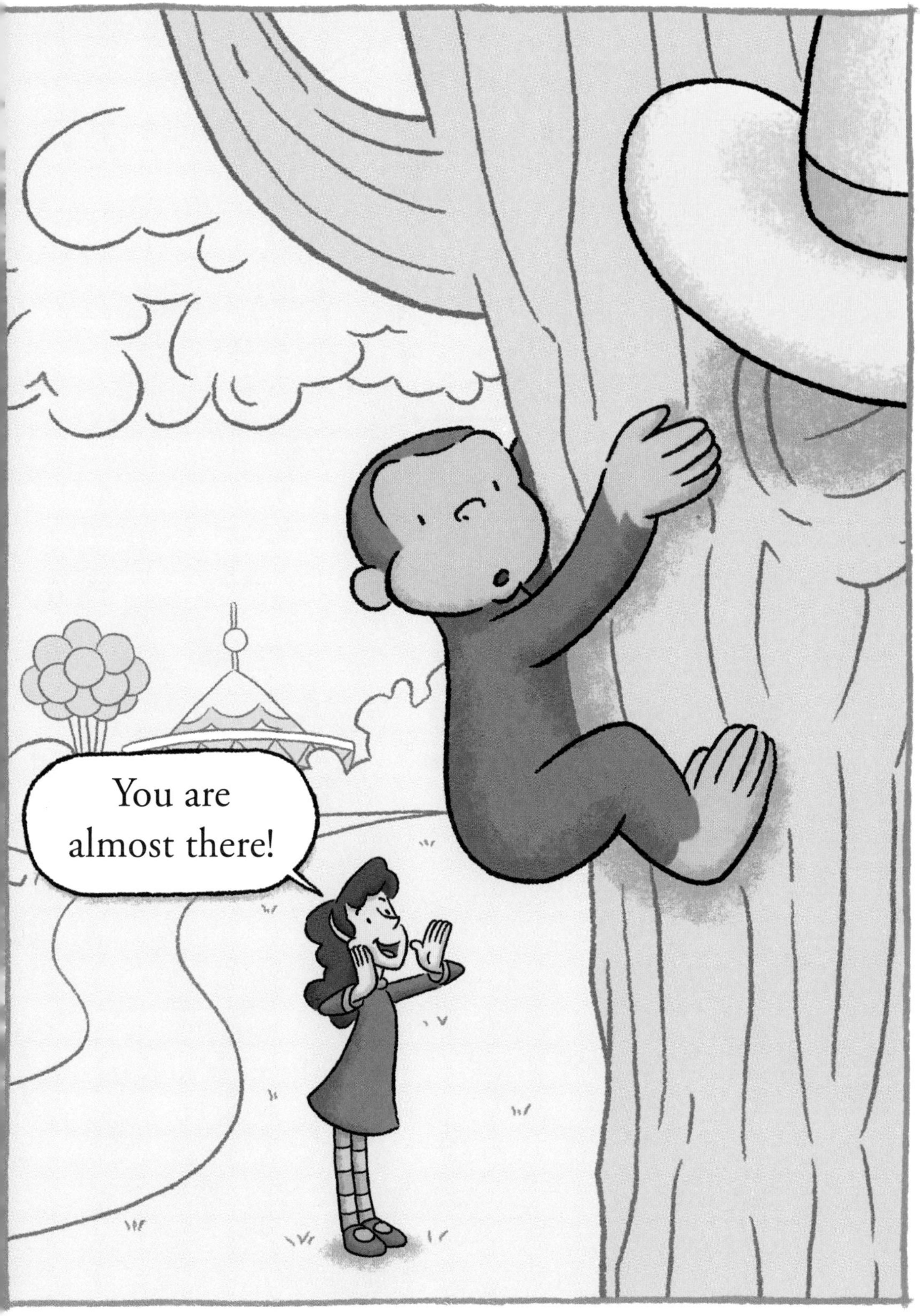
You are almost there!

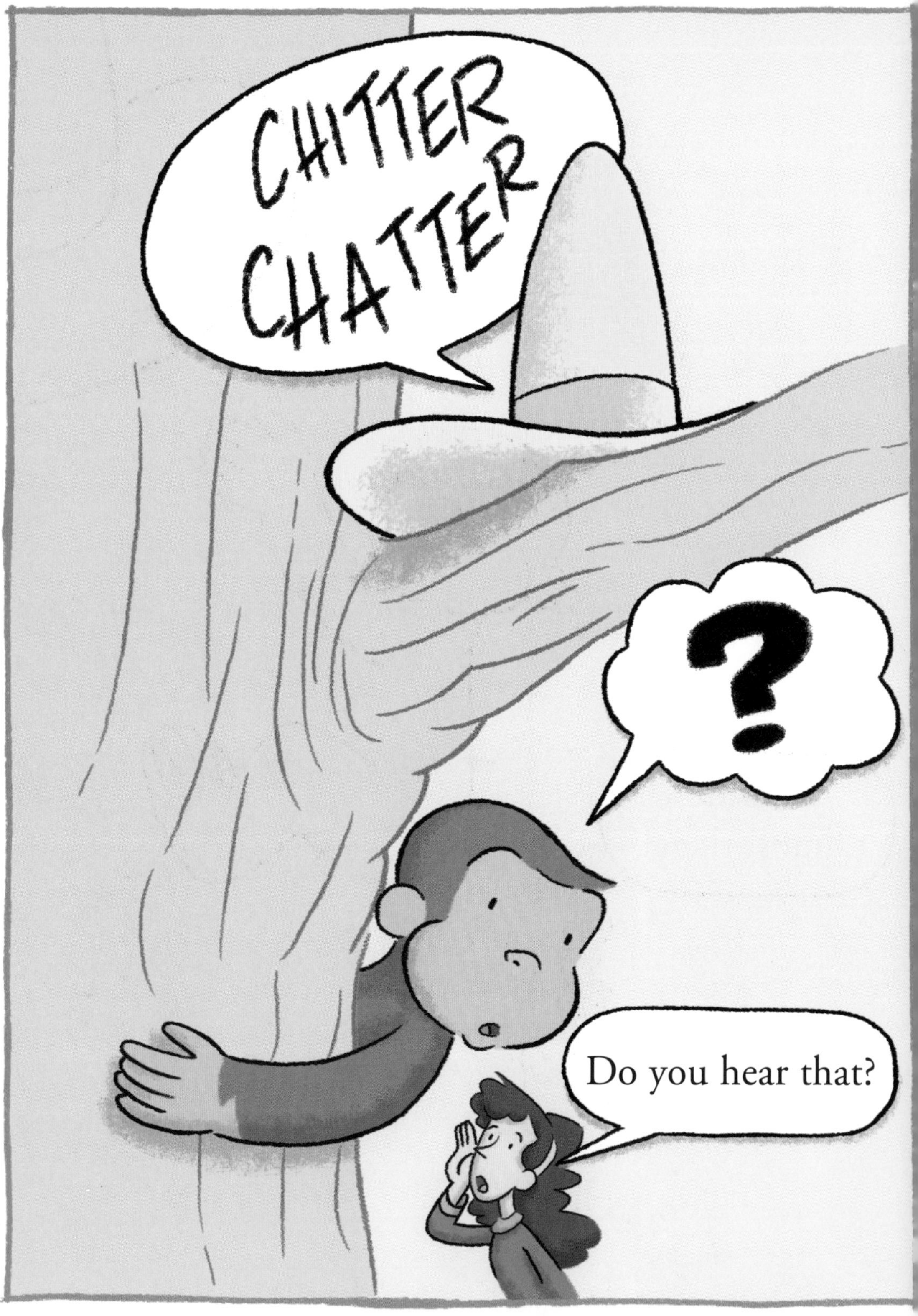
CHITTER CHATTER
?
Do you hear that?

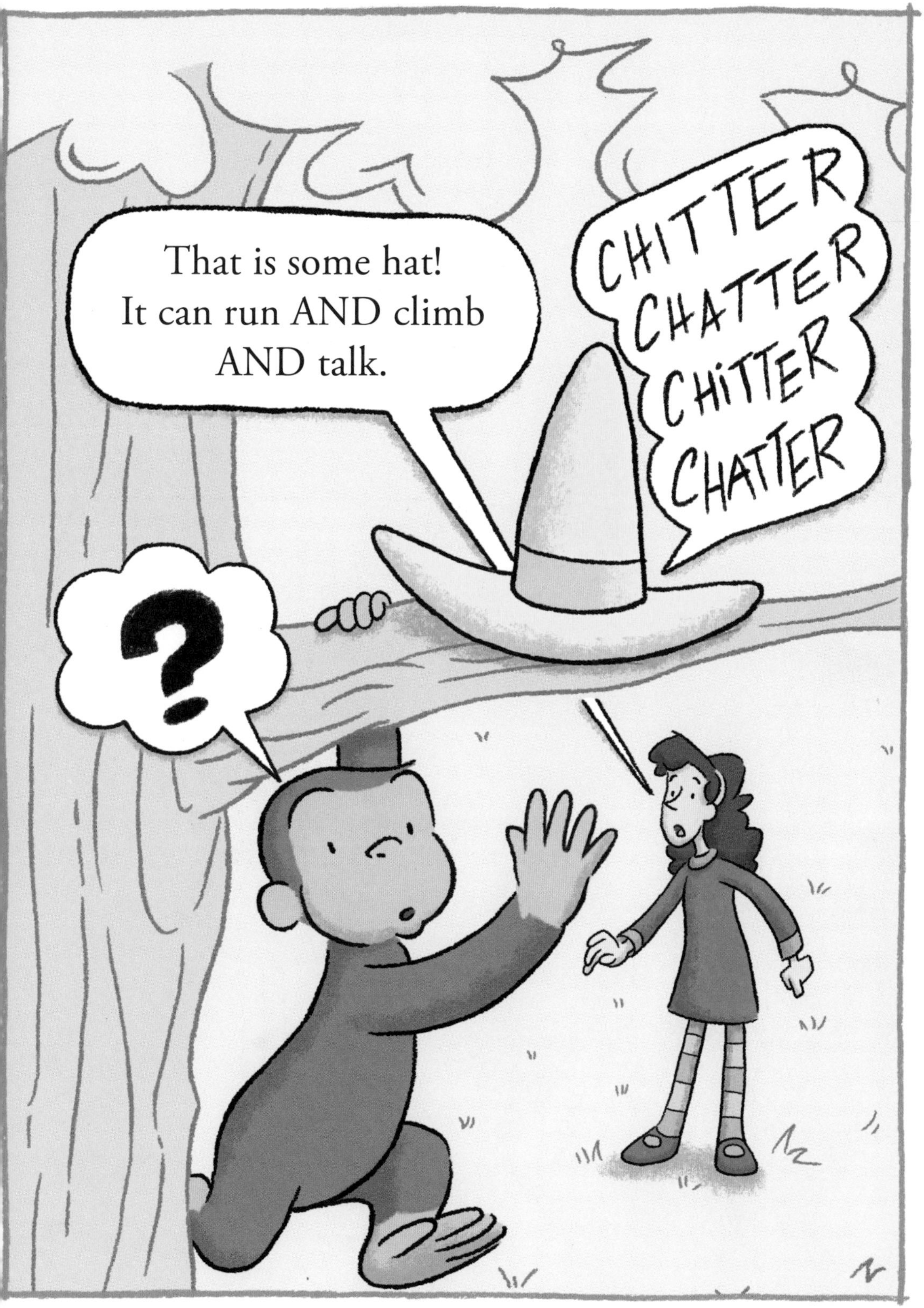
That is some hat!
It can run AND climb
AND talk.
CHITTER CHATTER CHITTER CHATTER
?

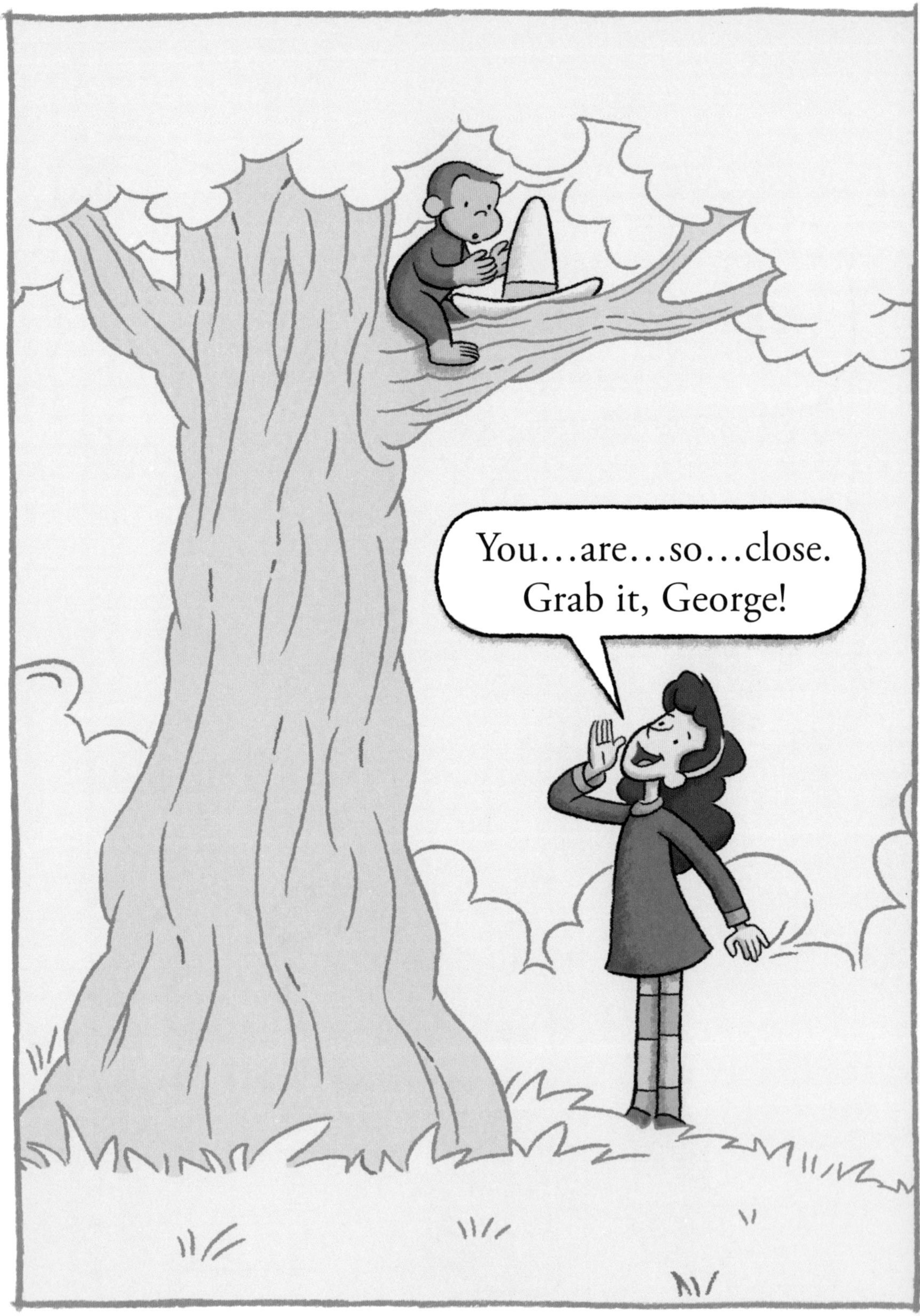
You…are…so…close.
Grab it, George!

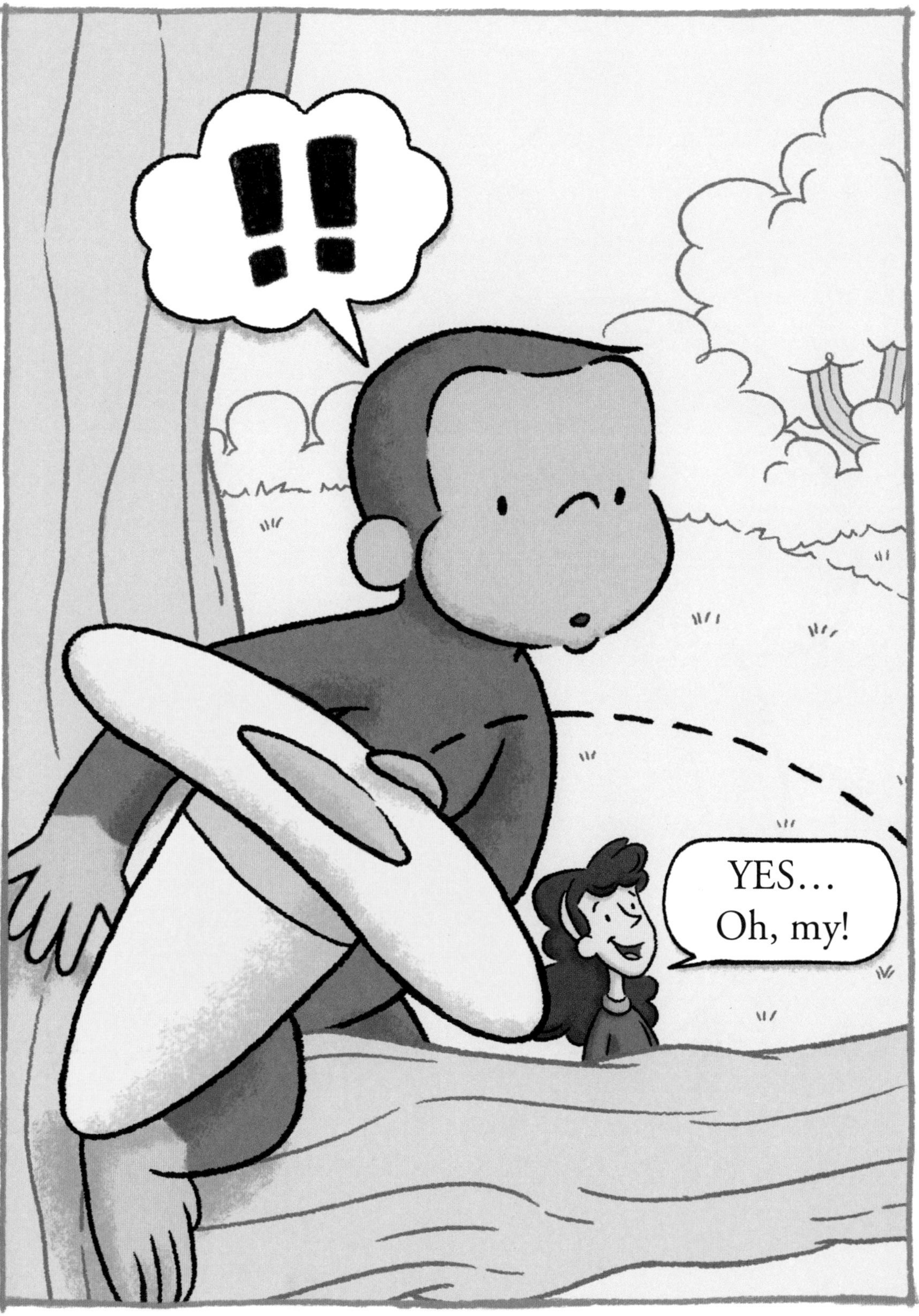
!!
YES…
Oh, my!

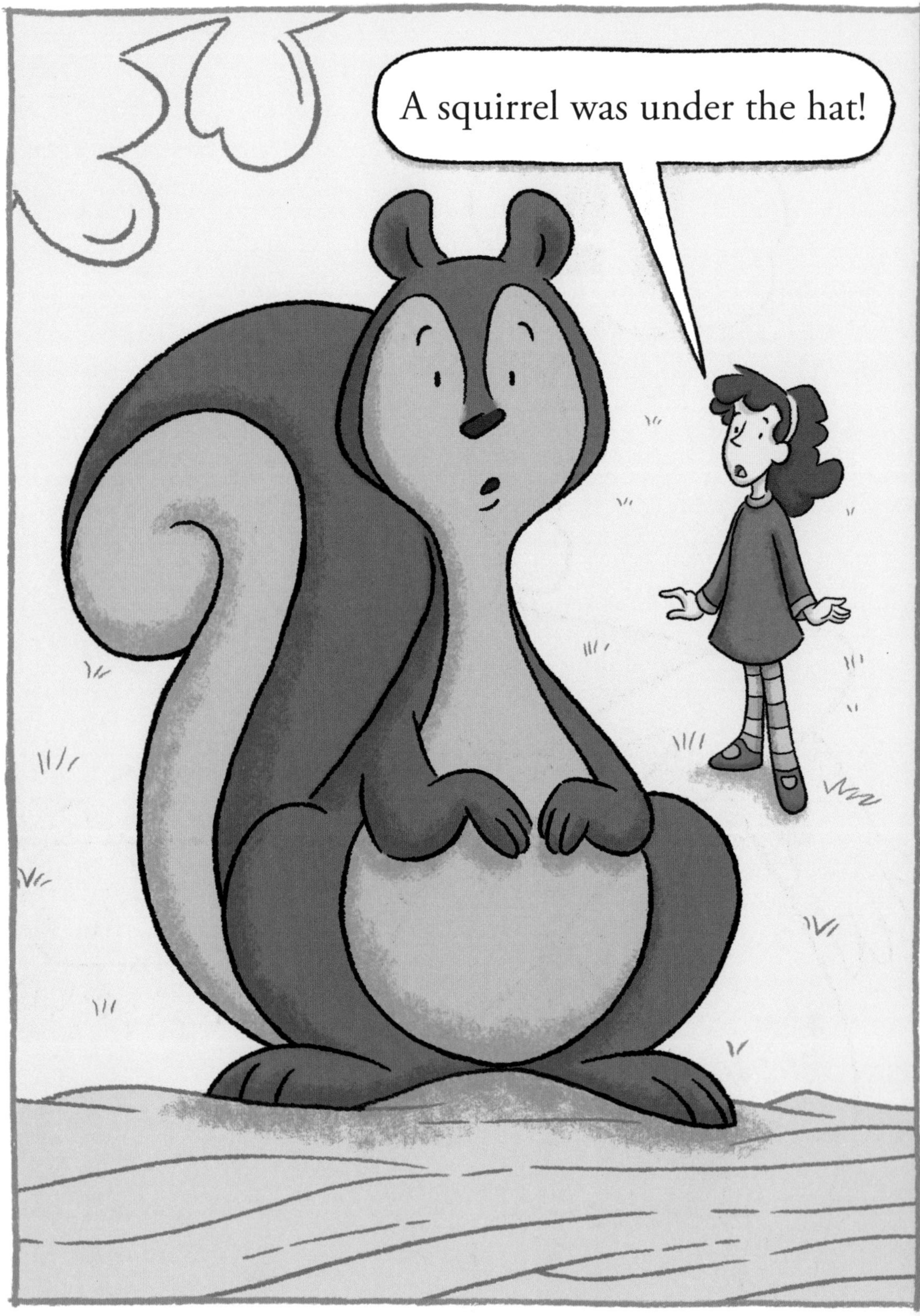
A squirrel was under the hat!

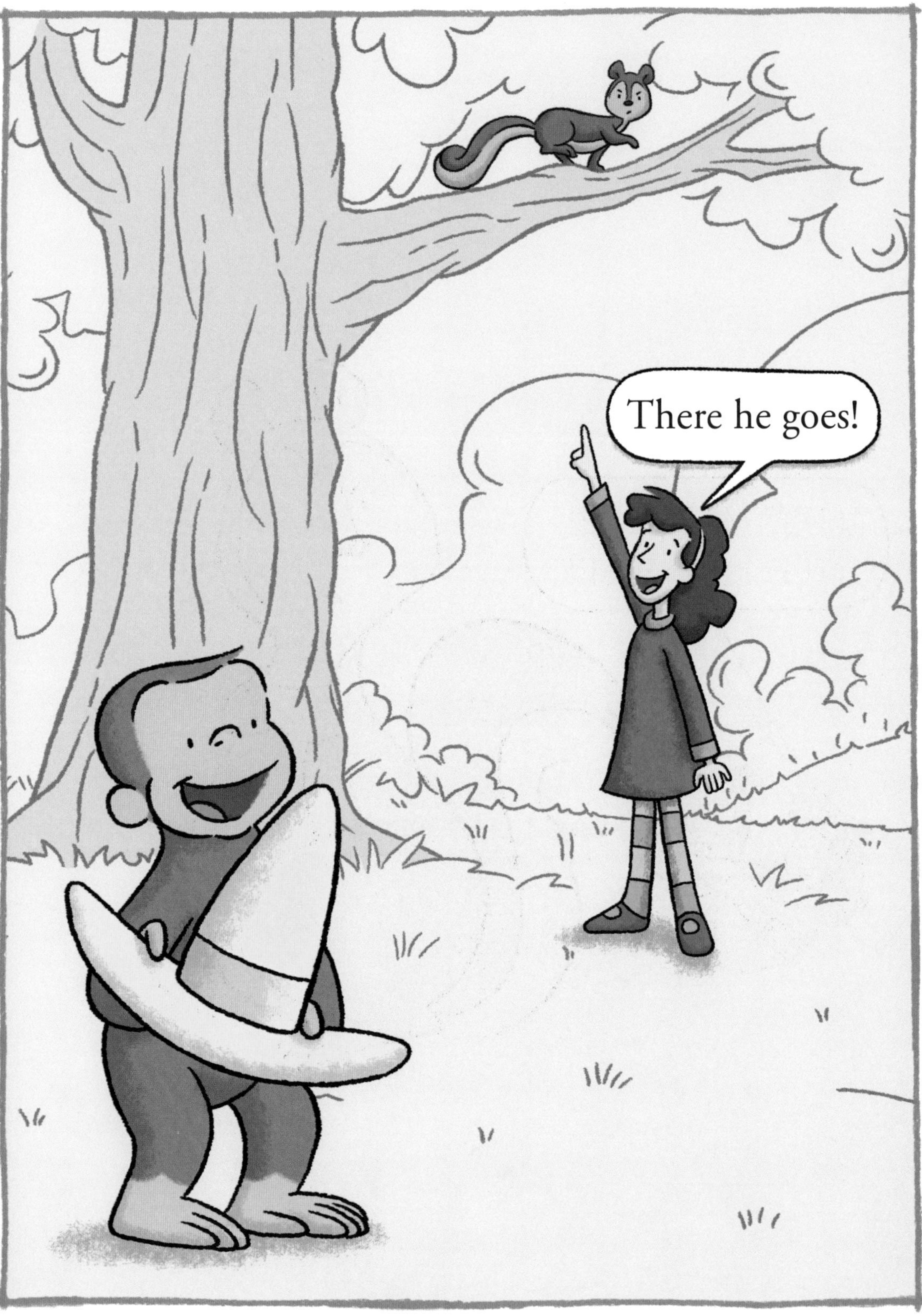
There he goes!

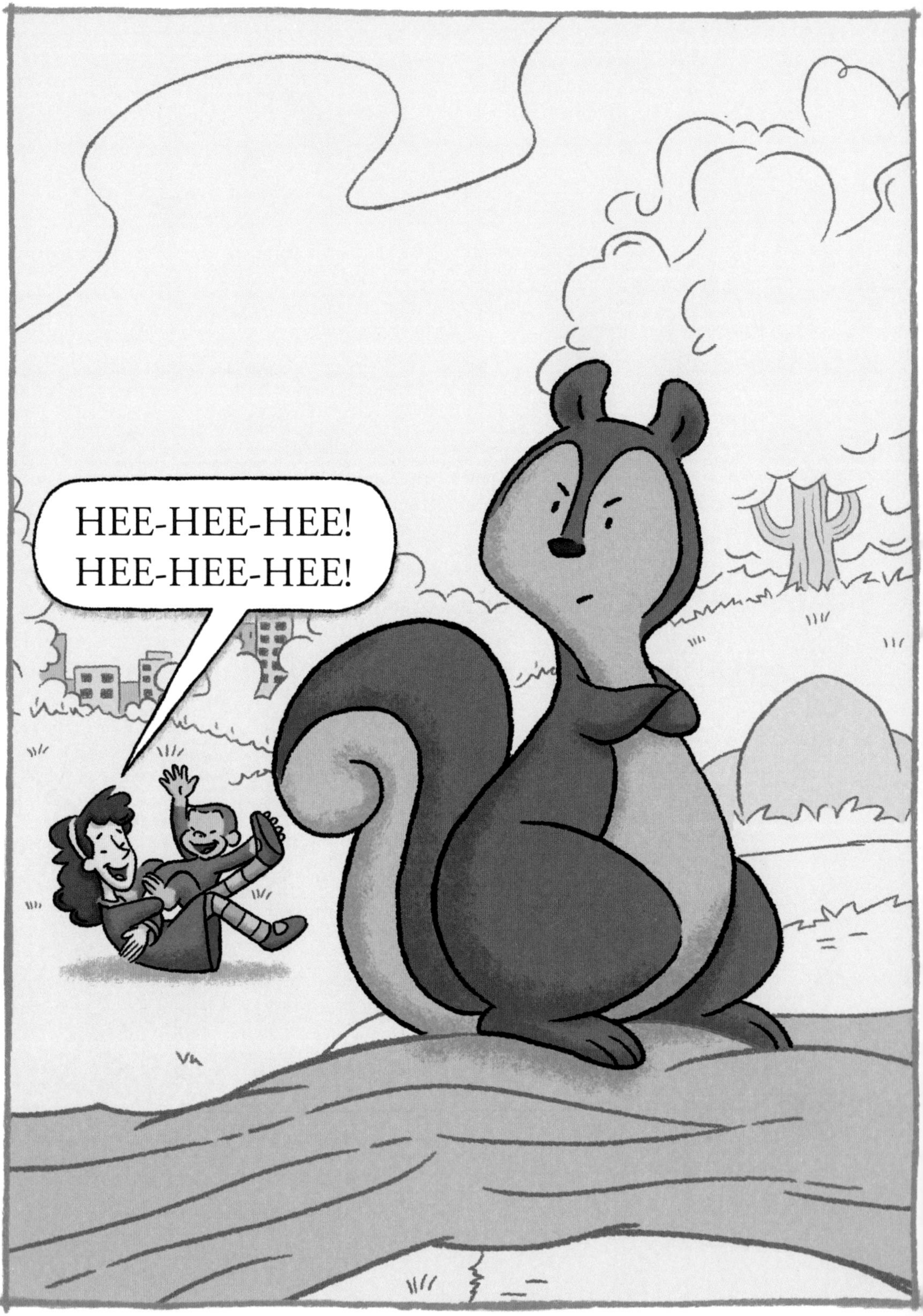
HEE-HEE-HEE!
HEE-HEE-HEE!

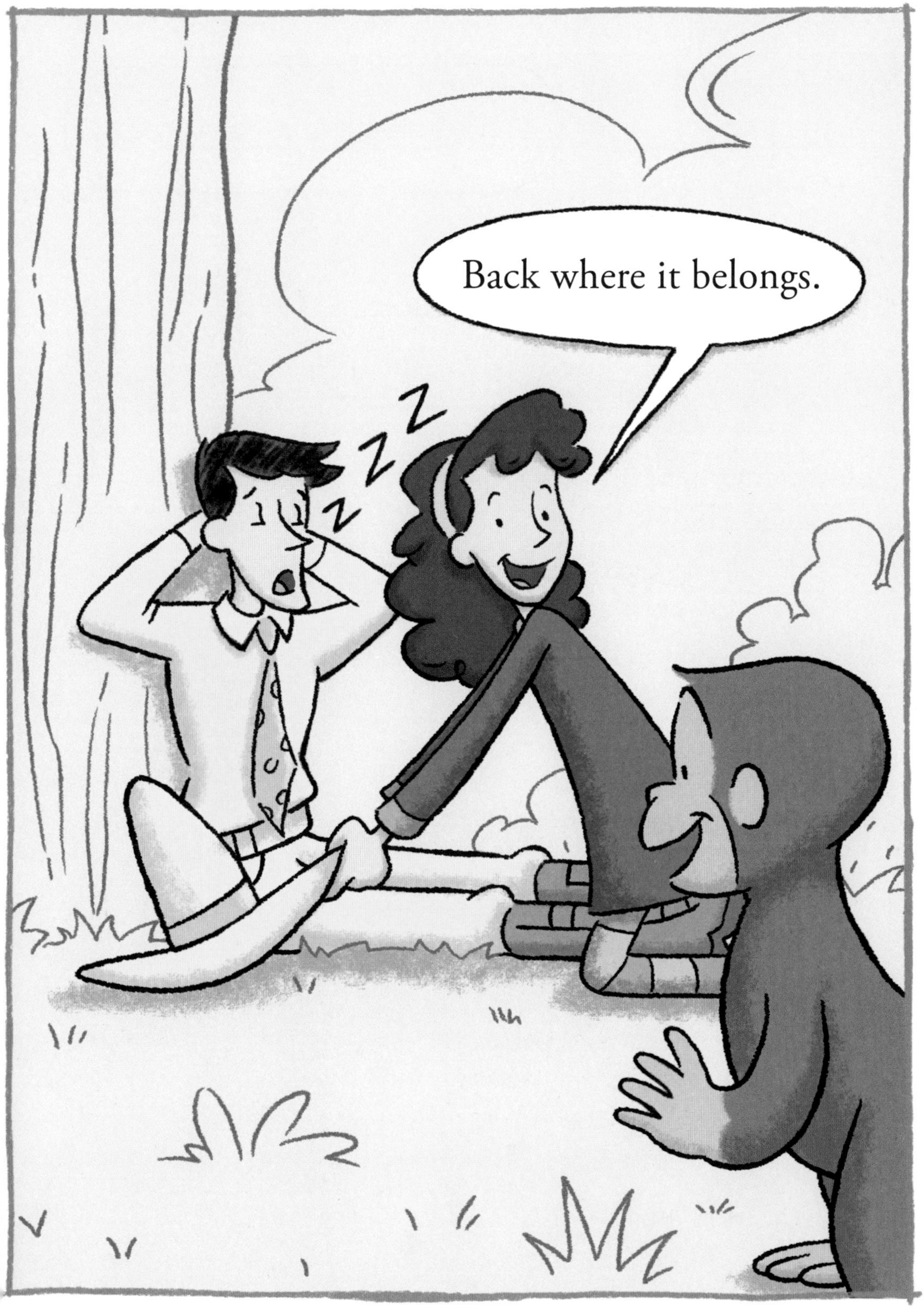
Back where it belongs.
ZZZZ

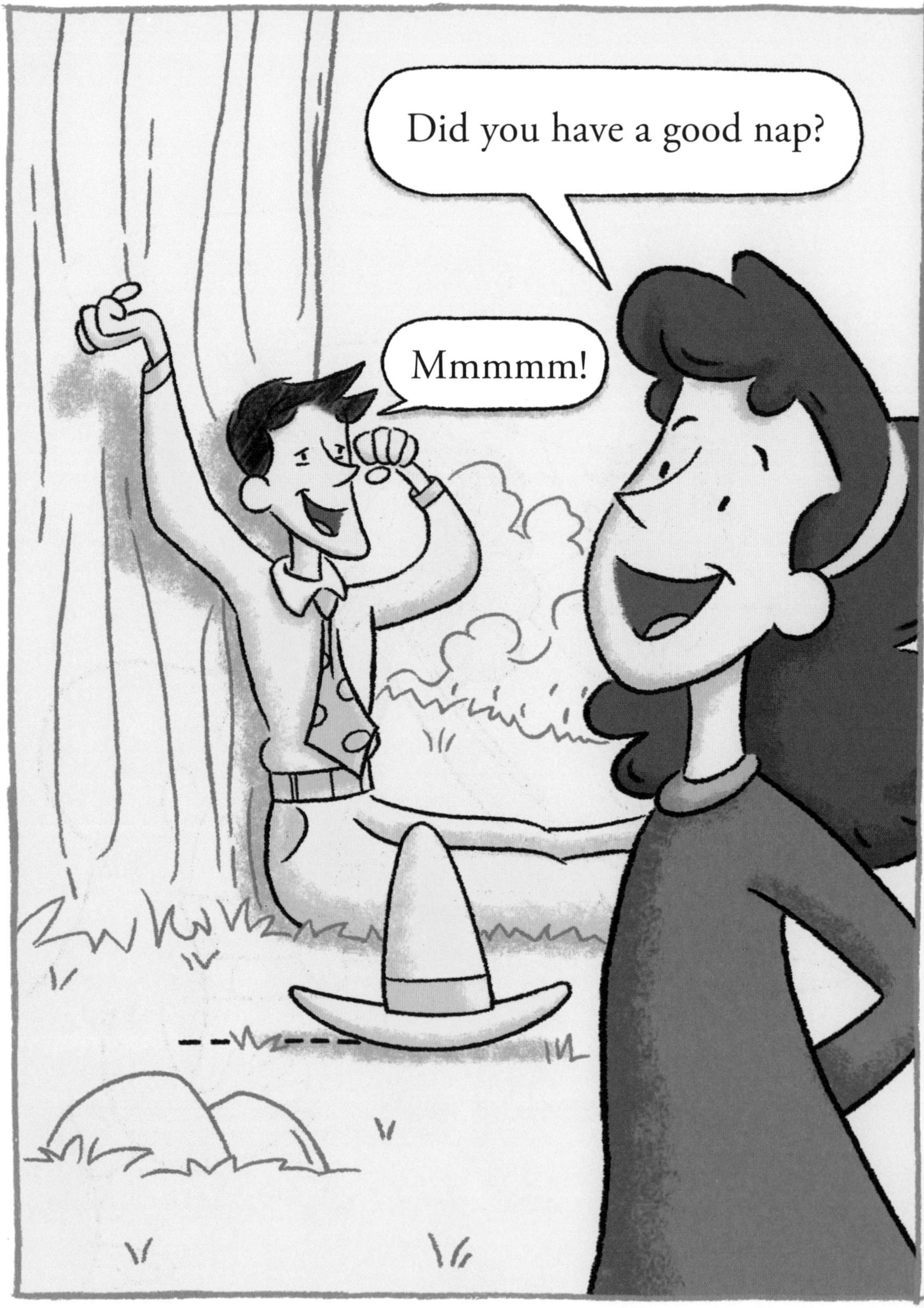
Did you have a good nap?
Mmmmm!

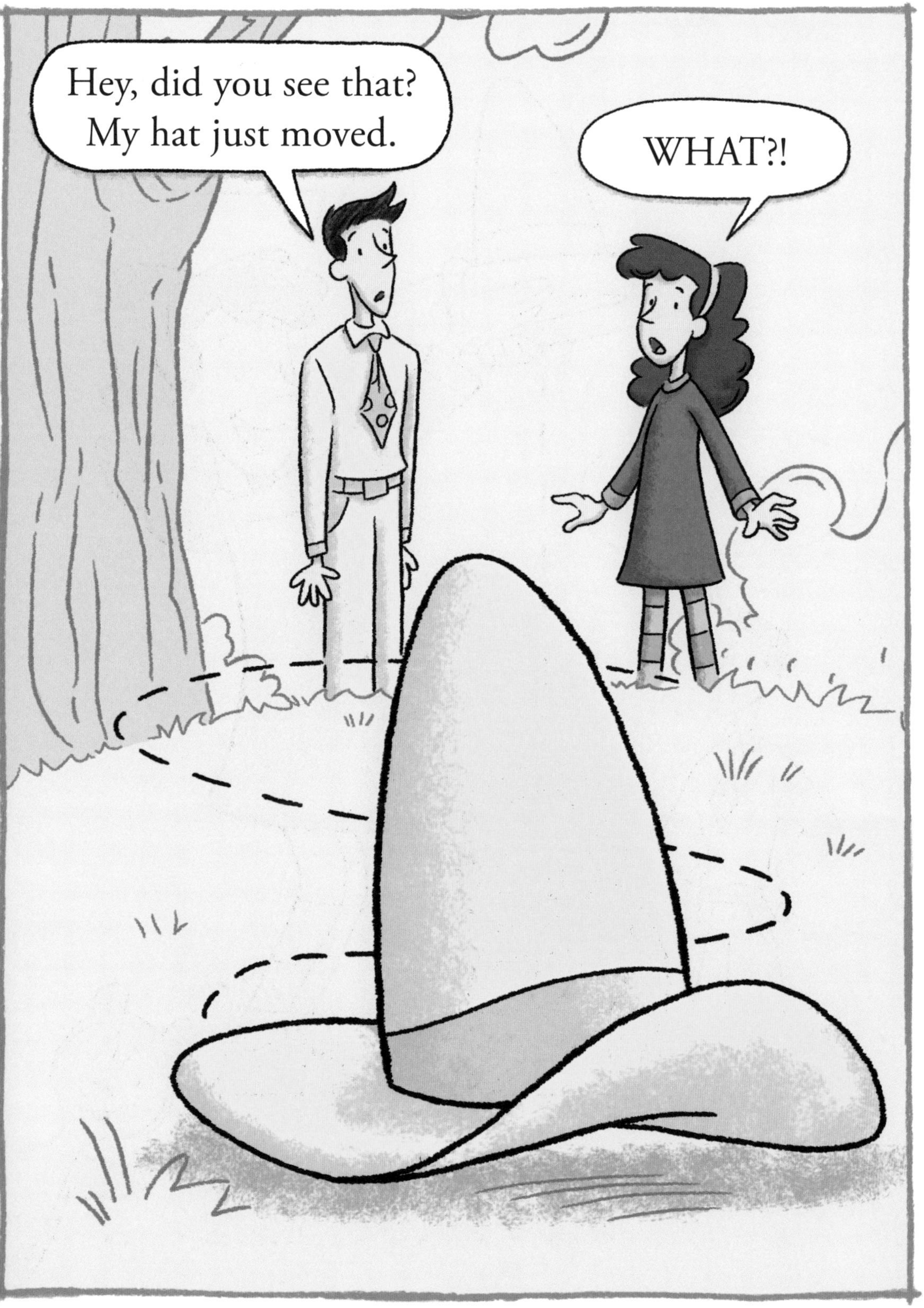
Hey, did you see that? My hat just moved.
WHAT?!

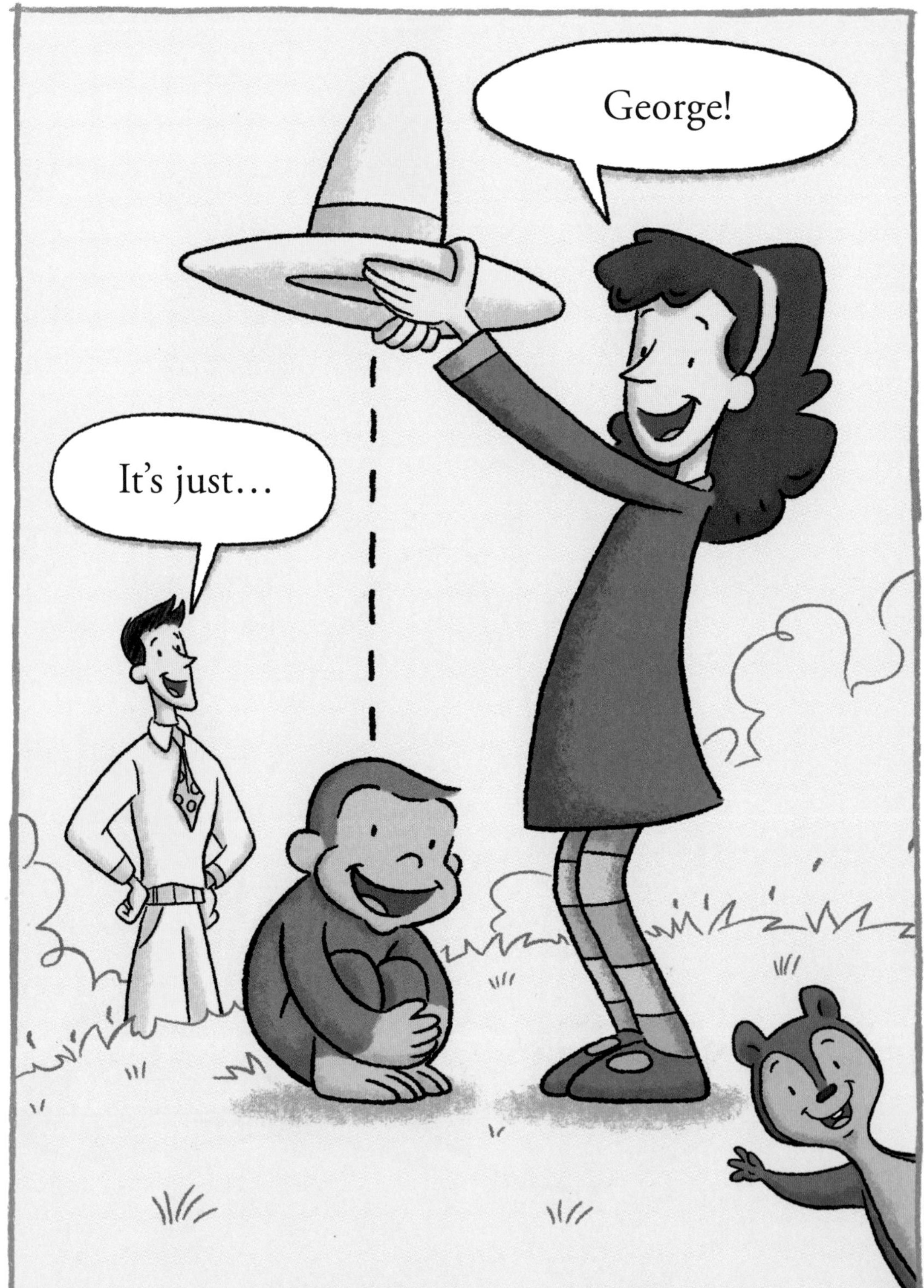
George!
It's just…

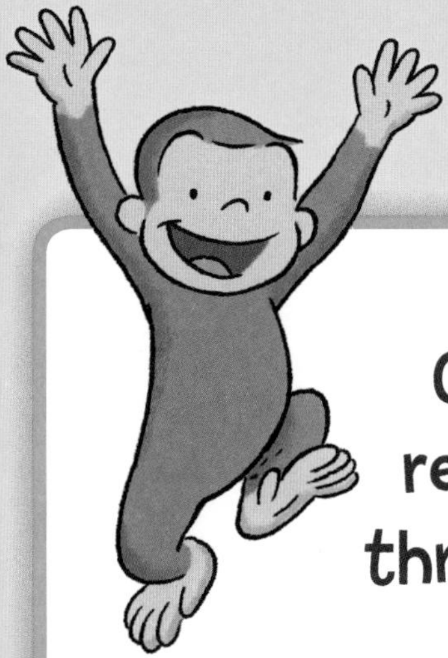

Get your child ready to read in three simple steps!

1 I READ	Read the book to your child.
2 WE READ	Read the book together.
3 YOU READ	Encourage your child to read the book over and over again.

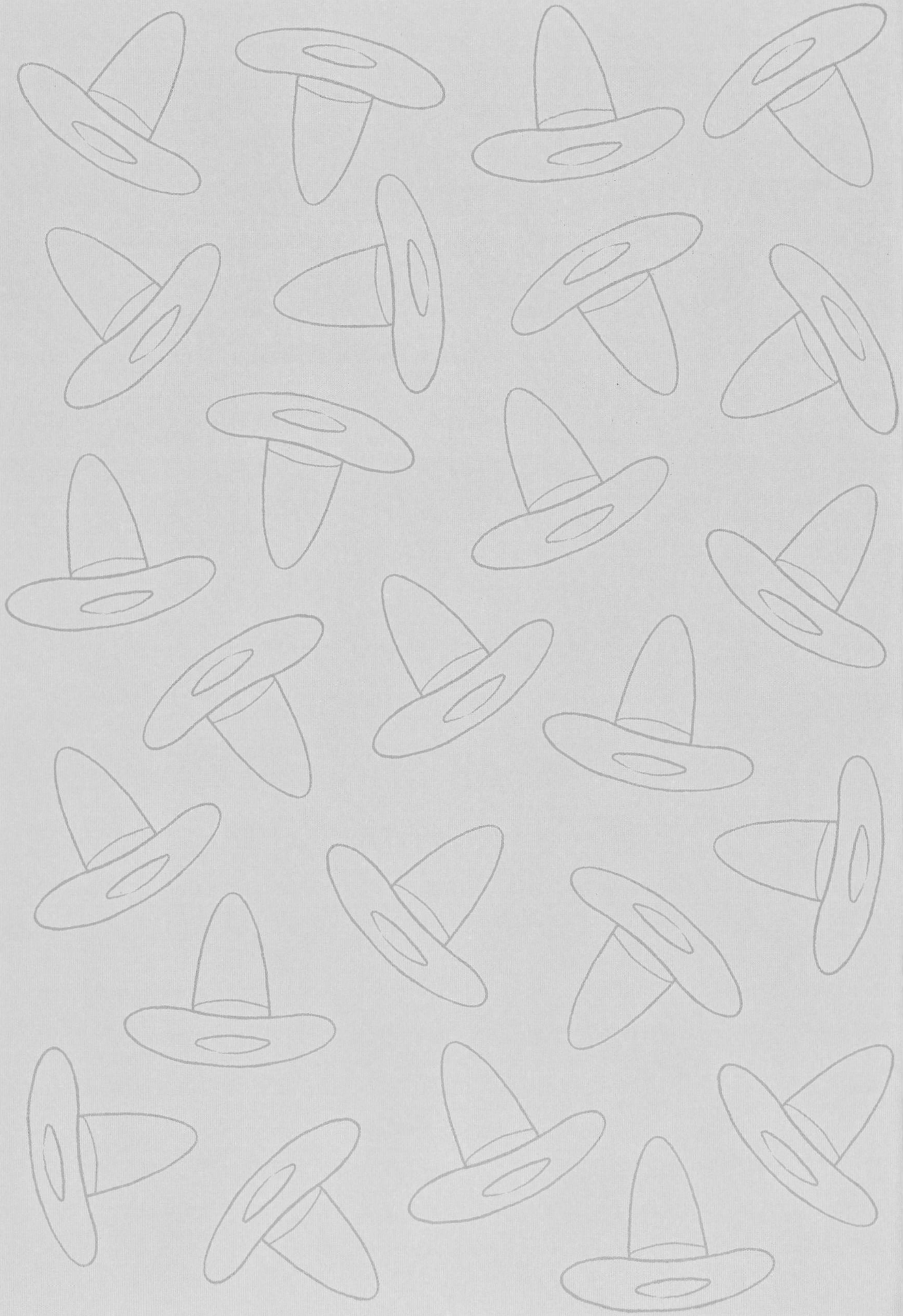

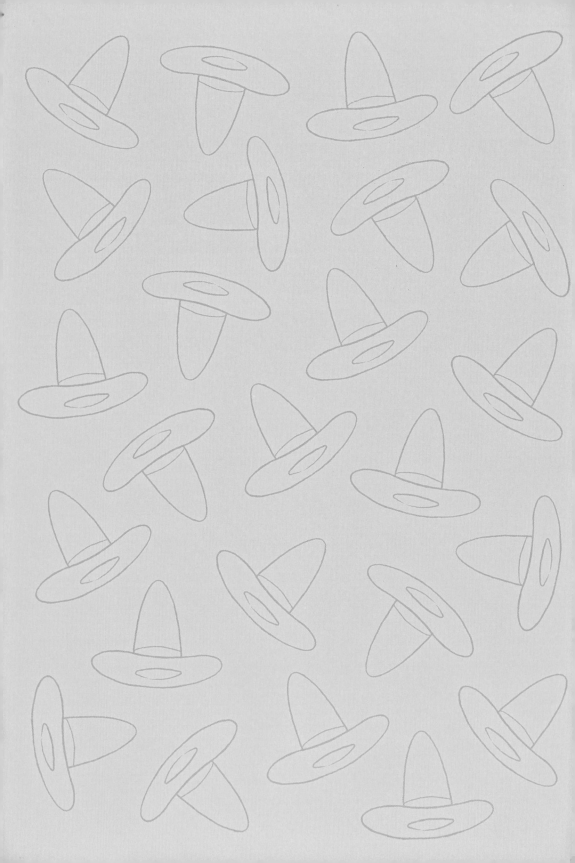